THE SHAME OF MIDDLE GRATESTONE

By Shaun Armstrong

To my family for their patience and support. To Al and Sarah for their time and valuable advice.

Table of Contents

Chapter 1

10th of January 1916

Alfred swept the slices of bread off the kitchen table and kicked them underneath. They should be safe there until he could retrieve them in the dead of night... if the rats didn't sniff them out first. His stomach grumbled at being made to wait.

He looked around, he still had time. On the worktop he could see potato peelings, they were no doubt going to be fed to the pigs rather than be used to thicken the orphans' weak broth. Alfred stuffed some peelings into his pockets, he could share them out to the other children later for them to chew in bed.

Satisfied with his haul Alfred grabbed the dishcloth that he had been sent to collect then turned and walked straight into George Edmund, the manager of the Middle Gratestone poorhouse on Church Road.

"I got the cloth," Alfred held it up as evidence, hoping he hadn't been spotted.

"Thief!" George Edmund spat. He grabbed Alfred by the back of the neck and yanked him around like a puppet, while pulling the peelings from Alfred's pockets. "I knew you were stealing food, now I've caught you." George Edmund dragged Alfred into the poorhouse long room past the table at which the other children were sat, thrust him outside into the cold and slammed the oak door shut.

"Horrible creature!" he yelled through the closed door. Then swivelled his eyes, hunting a new target.

"You're always whining and needing things, you always want more, you should be happy with what you've got," he seethed at the children sat at the table, venting his fury on them, now that he had ejected the source of his anger from the poorhouse. The children looked down in unison, too fearful to meet his eye, and presented him with a view of anonymous, messy hair.

"Don't spill any of that broth or you'll be licking it off the floor," he warned. So, they all remained head down, and shovelled the stew in the wooden bowls in front of them into their hungry mouths. George Edmund paced around the table on the freshly scrubbed flagstones, lost in his angry thoughts.

"How dare that swine steal from me?" he said indignantly as a bulbous vein pulsed at his temple. He walked up to the table, while the children raced to finish their food before it was taken away. "How dare he steal from you?" he looked down at the table trying to unite the children against the thief. "The food in the kitchen was yours, and he took it!" he goaded.

The children already knew that Alfred had been stealing food from the kitchen. At night, in the cold damp dormitory, he padded around silently in bare feet and shared out his ill-gotten scraps. The children took the food in grateful silence and ate quietly under their thin itchy blankets. It didn't matter what Alfred found for them, a bite of raw potato, a mouthful of bread, a cold wet vegetable boiled beyond recognition and fished from the cooking pot, nothing was too inedible for the hungry children. For weeks, Alfred's efforts had kept their strength up. He had risked everything for them, but now that he was being banished, they looked down and hid their faces in fear.

Most of them were younger than Alfred and had suffered the hardship of the poorhouse for longer. They were beaten, spiritless and frightened, left without the confidence to protest or the initiative to run. They wore wretchedness as a disguise, to hide any happiness left within them and prevent it being beaten out by George Edmund's overused leather belt. Banishment from the poorhouse for them, in the grip of winter, would result in death. They knew it, so they looked down, hid their faces, and were thankful for the weak watery broth that they continued to shovel into their hungry mouths.

Only one child, frail from persistent sickness, and stunted by ill health, peeked up at the door and mourned Alfred's departure. Alfred had been his protector all his life and without him his world suddenly seemed lonely and empty. Perhaps George Edmund would relent and let Alfred back in shortly, he hoped and looked back down.

"Horrible creature! Good riddance!" George Edmund shouted at the door. "I hope you freeze!" he added spitefully, his face contorting in rage. Spittle flecked his lips and flew from his mouth to land in the hair of the nearest children. They didn't flinch though, for fear of violent reprisal. "Better to freeze than starve," George Edmund said under his breath and shuffled off to do what he considered was Christian business.

Outside, Alfred paused with the poorhouse door at his back. He was protected for now, from the cold winter wind that stirred the poorhouse rubbish on the broken stone slabs that formed the path to a broken gate. The gate banged and creaked rhythmically in the wind, while the poorhouse rubbish danced in neat circles partnered by brown leaves. Alfred stood still, watching the rubbish that like himself had been thrown from the poorhouse, and started to form a plan. He looked to the sky, it was a cold windy day, the temperature was not much above freezing, and dark clouds were racing in.

"I wish I'd packed," he commented to the wind. The wind carried his words away.

Alfred was not best prepared. He was dressed in thin threadbare trousers, tied at the waist with rope scavenged from the canal, and a thin cotton shirt, tucked into the trousers and held in place by the rope. The ragged cuffs were rolled up and the shirt was too large for his lean frame. The buttons running down the front were all different shapes and sizes because they had been lost and replaced over the years, and it was now unclear which if any were original. He was a good-looking boy, lean from malnourishment, but strong from hard work, and tall for his thirteen-years-of-age. He had a confident look about him and large hands and feet. In time he would grow into a strong able man.

The banging gate drew Alfred's attention. Next to the gate, he spied a package in brown paper, tied up with string that crossed at the top and finished in a neat bow. Packages were often left at the gate for the poorhouse orphans. They contained the townsfolk's unwanted belongings and served to soothe their gnawing consciences. Alfred walked over to the gate, grabbed the package by the string, and bolted.

He ran to the church nearby, jumped the low, neat, stone wall that circled around the church graveyard, and hid behind a gravestone to be out of view from townsfolk passing by. Leaning back on the gravestone, he worked quickly for fear of discovery.

Inside the package he found an old nightshirt, two pairs of knitted socks and an old flat cap. He put the night shirt on under his own shirt, shivering in the cold as he undressed and dressed, and tucked its long length into his trousers. It was baggy and much too big for him, but his own shirt held it in place and concealed its nocturnal purpose.

He took his boots off, one at a time, and placed one pair of the wool socks over his own holed socks and put his boots back on. They were good sturdy boots that once were two sizes too big but now fitted well. One had no lace so he used the string to tie the boot securely in place.

The other pair of socks he pulled over his hands, and wiggled his fingers to himself in satisfaction. Gloves were hard to come by, but socks were commonplace, he had used this method before and it would keep his hands warm.

Cold was no stranger to Alfred, cold had been his companion many times before; he had slept with cold, eaten with cold, and worked and walked with cold. Cold had never beaten him and he was determined that it would not beat him today. He looked at the brown paper that the clothes had been wrapped in. It was his only possession so reluctant to cast it aside, he stood up and stuffed it down the back of his trousers.

“No sense in a cold bum,” he congratulated himself with a cheery smile and set off out of the graveyard, pausing by three new gravestones before he left. They gleamed white and held his attention for a moment–finally he stood straight, saluted to the gravestones in military fashion, and hopped over the low stone wall.

Chapter 2

11th of January 2016

The snow that had secretly fallen under the cover of darkness, had left the town of Middle Gratestone, cold and shivering under a thick white blanket. It was morning, but the sun still lingered below the horizon and had not yet revealed the pristine white covering to the town's inhabitants. Orange tinted clouds, unburdened of their heavy load, had scattered under the gentle insistence of a light breeze and the sky slowly lightened from black to blue. Just one or two stubborn stars still resisted daybreak and defiantly attempted to lengthen the winter night.

Jane was out early. She took big exaggerated steps to ease her way through the heavy drifts that lay on the path. They were banked up here and there, thrown by a disorderly wind against walls and houses, and slowed Jane's progress. The leafless trees that lined the road, bore the snow on branches bent in protest. Jane kept a watchful eye and ducked under the lowest, taking care not to touch them for fear of dislodging a freezing white shower. The sound of the wakening town was deadened by the thick drifts; only Jane's strong, even breathing broke the silence. She clutched her schoolbag to her middle, hoping to gain warmth from it, and pushed on towards the comfort of the classroom and chatter of her friends.

Jane didn't care much at all for this part of her walk to school and refused to look at the graveyard, next to the path, behind the low stone wall. The graveyard surrounded an old church that had a grey slate roof and lofty bell tower, the walls were darkened with age and looked black in the dim morning light.

A weathervane spiked the top of the bell tower and creaked in complaint as it was teased by the indecisive breeze. Gravestones, set in unmoving stone ranks, surrounded the church and marked where the dead lay. The more ancient of the gravestones had succumbed to injuries inflicted by time and weather, and crumbled to the ground.

Jane looked across the narrow tree lined road, away from the graveyard and church with its black walls, towards the terrace of brightly coloured cottages where soft light glowed through still closed curtains. She imagined the people inside getting ready to start their day.

A cup of tea and toast for the old white-haired gentleman at number three, fruit and perhaps something continental for the young couple at number five, and a full English for the large gentleman at number seven, who often heralded his departure from home with the most awful trumpeted wind. He had troubled himself to name his home 'Thatcher's Rest' on a garish yellow plaque mounted high near the front door, it clashed horribly with the bright orange walls but somehow seemed to fit in with the myriad of colours adorning the other cottages. In the spring, window boxes and gardens full of flowers, competed with the painted walls and attracted bees that buzzed in harmony as they appeared and disappeared amongst the petals and leaves. For now, though, winter held fast, and the gardens remained a hidden memory buried deep under the snow.

It was this forced preoccupation with the cottages that prevented Jane from noticing something unusual in the graveyard. Amongst the ranks of snow topped gravestones and white capped statues, one statue of a boy dressed in rags stood out. He stood slightly apart, facing the path along which Jane walked and watched her progress with cold stone eyes. The statue was kneeling on a stone plinth, with its arms outstretched as if pleading. He was made from a black, smooth stone that glistened wet from the snow that had melted on the surface, his black, curly hair, a dark hood amongst the white crowned angels and cherubs that watched over the dead.

Had Jane noticed, she may have puzzled over why the snow had laid on all the statues except this one. Of course, Jane had seen the statue before, and knew the story behind it which is why she feared catching the statue's cold stone eye, and why she always looked away from the graveyard towards the colourful cottages. The boy was called Alfred, but he was more often referred to as, the shame of Middle Gratestone.

Chapter 3

10th of January 1916

Alfred looked up and down Church Road. He was alone. Everyone who had a choice had been driven inside by the sudden freeze. Smoke from warming fires billowed from nearby chimneys and was blown sideways in parallel tracks underneath the grey threatening clouds. A chill wind stirred leafless branches causing them to chatter nervously against each other, and rustling bushes whispered of snow. Dusk was approaching and it was bringing cold and hardship for Alfred with it.

The people of Middle Gratestone sheltered behind the stone walls of their homes, stoking fires and preparing supper. Tonight, was a night for families to huddle up under blankets, by the fire, and share stories over warm tea.

Alfred surveyed the scene and weighed his options. He was not worried about shelter. He knew this area well, including the nooks and crannies where he could hide out. He had lived here once, back when his life had been different, and he knew which households locked their doors and which didn't. He thought that if he carried out night time raids, and took just a little food from each house, he probably wouldn't be discovered. He didn't want to steal but it might be necessary for a while.

A distant hooter sounded, it announced to the town that work at the paper factory was finished for the day. The local policeman would be out watching and talking with the workers as they left, so Alfred decided to lie low and wait for darkness to provide him shadows in which to move.

He did not trust the policeman. The policeman had been involved in everything bad that had happened in Alfred's life and Alfred had fought several times with the policeman's son. The policeman did not much like Alfred either. Alfred knew that attention from the police would only mean more trouble, so he decided to keep himself hidden.

There was a den that he and his brothers had built in the woods, behind the cottages on Church Road. Before he had been forced to hand himself in at the poorhouse, he had hidden some essentials there in an old cake tin. Today seemed to be just the kind of day that he had been saving for. With one last look around the deserted road, he crossed over and headed into the wood through the dense undergrowth, completely unaware that unfriendly eyes were watching.

He followed the small animal trails that cut through and crisscrossed the bushes and brambles that covered the ground underneath the trees. Sometimes walking, and sometimes crawling, he made it through the maze of tracks to the centre.

Two large trees had fallen, blown over in a long-ago storm, creating a clearing right in the heart of the wood. Their thick, gnarled trunks lay on the ground parallel to each other, creating a barrier that reached Alfred's shoulder. They were covered in branches and brush, and looked impassable. Alfred walked down towards the thicker end of the nearest fallen tree–its broken roots fanned out and pointed accusingly up at the clouds above, as if blaming them for its violent end.

He pulled back a piece of loose brush and squeezed through the roots. Inside, between the two great tree trunks, was a cleared area where many fires had been lit. Towards the back, wooden planks had been nailed to create a covered area, long and wide enough for two or three people to lie down in, and on top of them lay the branches and brush that were visible from the outside.

Alfred set about clearing out anything wet and finding some dry brush and kindling. Large dry logs were stacked at the back of the hideout, these would provide warmth for many nights. Once everything was in order, he stood silently and listened to the sound of the woodland. His older brother had taught him this routine–to always listen before lighting a fire. Every woodland had a natural sound level, birds sang, and small creatures rustled around in the brown leaves that littered the ground. Alfred was well hidden from view, but a fire would be visible to anyone in the immediate vicinity. He waited patiently for any sound that might indicate someone was in the area, and tuned his senses to the woodland around him.

Finally, satisfied that no one else was there, he ducked down into the hideout and scratched around in a crevice under one of the tree trunks. After a short search he found what he was looking for. Carefully, he pulled out an old cake tin, rusted here and there, and dirty with earth. Alfred brushed the earth off from around the lid, and pried it off with his short, dirty fingernails. He took out a flint, and then replaced the lid and hid the cake tin back under the tree trunk.

'Always be ready to flee' his older brother had told him, Alfred recalled, 'never leave anything out that you cannot run with.'

Alfred took the piece of wrapping paper from out of the back of his trousers, and tore a strip off, before replacing the remainder back in its warm hiding place. He knelt on the floor, tore the strip into smaller pieces and mixed them with small dry twigs and brush to form kindling. He placed the kindling in front of him and then started to work the flint. The sparks were bright in the gloom and landed in the kindling which immediately glowed and smouldered. Alfred picked it up, closed his hand around it, and blew softly. The kindling caught fire and lit his face with an orange glow. With great satisfaction, Alfred placed the kindling down gently and began to build a fire around it, using first small twigs and then larger sticks and finally some logs. Slowly, as the fire caught and flickered into life, throwing shadows on the knotted tree trunk, Alfred began to feel warm and safe. He kept the fire small so that light and sparks were not thrown into the night sky and the smoke and smell did not drift outside of the wood.

Alfred looked up, large snowflakes were starting to fall from the night sky, they appeared golden in the light from the fire, and floated down gracefully. He stuck his tongue out, and for a happy hour, caught them in his mouth as they drifted within reach, for a short while, the void inside him that had been created by the loss of his mother and father, was filled with fun and concentration. Slowly though, as tiredness overcame him, he stopped catching the snowflakes and instead let them land and melt on his flat cap. He stared straight forward and became lost in thought as the flames danced and snowflakes hissed in surprise as they dropped into the fire.

He started to think about the things that he always thought of when sleep tugged at him and eroded his resolve not to dwell on the past. Why had his father left him to go to war? He had been there when his father left, they all hugged him and they all cried, except Father, he never cried. Alfred had looked at him on that day, and he thought his father wasn't even sad. He tried to be sad of course but every now and then a smile would appear and he looked excited as if he was looking forward to going.

'It's my duty,' he had said to Alfred, but Alfred always thought it was more than that. Alfred had always thought that his father had wanted to go, and Alfred hated himself because of it. Perhaps he should have been a better son. He was thirteen years old and should have been more help than hindrance. Perhaps if he had worked harder, his father would have wanted to stay. The feeling of anger and resentment was always with him. Alfred could feel it despite all his efforts to push it away. He tried to help other people, to stop the anger eating at him, that was why he stole food in the poorhouse and gave it to the other children. For a while this would cause the pain to subside and he felt better about himself. A small gift of kindness given to someone else warmed him and gave him purpose. Alfred didn't want to be sad, he didn't want to hate, but he knew that even though an act of kindness eased the pain that he was broken inside. His heart and soul would never be well again, the pain and hatred he carried was too much, and he was on a path that would lead to personal ruin.

He remembered the day his mother received the two telegrams. They were delivered together by the vicar and the mayor. The post office had alerted them and they came in person to deliver the news. Alfred was there, and he saw his mother crushed as they read the telegrams out loud. He saw the joy go out of her eyes, as she was told her husband and eldest son were dead–killed in action in the war. He saw her sit in silence, after the vicar and mayor had left, and saw her still sat there in the same chair in the morning. All life had left her and she was cold and rigid. Her eyes were open and stared without seeing the cold fireplace.

Alfred went out to get the doctor. The doctor had come straight away but said there was nothing that he could do. Alfred's mother had passed away in the night and gone to heaven. In part, Alfred understood the loss and the hurt that his mother felt, because he felt it too. In part he understood the pain she felt and why her heart had broken. In part he understood that she had wanted to go to heaven to be with them. But what he didn't understand is why she had left him and little Alfred his younger brother. They were in pain as well. They needed her to reassure them and tell them it was going to be okay. They needed her to lie next to them at night and tell them the bad men wouldn't get them. They needed to know that heaven was real and that one day they would see their father and brother again. They needed love, care and affection. Their mother should have given it to them, but instead she had chosen death, and Alfred hated her for it. He didn't want to hate her, he just did. He wanted to love her, but he couldn't. Why had he and his little brother not been enough? It gnawed at his very heart and soul and changed him inside. He felt colder now, darker now, he felt angry and murderous.

His younger brother had stayed with him, and for a while they carried on as best they could at home in the cottage. They held hands and hugged, and talked all the time about everything except what had happened. Neighbours brought food to the cottage for them to eat and logs for the fire for them to warm themselves by, and for a month they survived. But then the policeman came and said they couldn't stay there anymore. Someone else was going to live there. The two boys were going to live with the other orphan children at the orphanage and be looked after by Mr Edmund. It didn't seem right to Alfred, but he didn't know what else to do, so two days later they left their home for the last time and went to stay with Mr Edmund.

The day that Alfred stepped into the poorhouse he hated himself, he hated his father and his mother, he hated the vicar and the mayor, he hated the policeman, and soon he would hate Mr Edmund. But for his brother, small and fragile at his side, Alfred hated everyone he knew.

With a sudden start, Alfred came back to reality, and realised he had been staring at the flames of his small fire swaying hypnotically in front of him. He was breathing hard and his fists were clenched so tight they were sore and strained. He relaxed again and tried to forget. His front was warm and dry from the fire, but his back was cold and stiff, the peak of his cap was wet from the melted snow where it stuck out from under the planks overhead. He shifted uncomfortably and looked through the fire, momentarily jerking in surprise as he saw the two eyes watching him from the other side. They were dark in the half light, and the fire was reflected in them. Alfred pushed himself up and backwards, banging his head on the planks as he did so, the blow stopped him from any further sudden movements and he froze and focused his gaze through the fire on the eyes that were still staring unblinking from the other side.

It's a dog, he thought seeing the pointed ears that stood up proud on top of the head and the long snout pointing at him, but then just as quickly, he realised it wasn't. It was a fox. It had beautiful blue eyes and was sat quietly on the other side of the fire watching Alfred as he drifted between unhappy memories and fitful dozing. They gazed at each other across the fire, neither one willing to move for fear of breaking the fires warm embrace, and neither one scared or aggressive. They held each other's gaze in silence.

Alfred relaxed, he was safe behind the fire, and if the fox was there then there must be no one else around. Despite himself, his mind began to drift again, his eyes grew heavy and sleep beckoned to him irresistibly. It had been a long time since he had slept by a fire, and his tiredness overwhelmed him as the fire crackled and kept the cold away, soon he drifted off.

Chapter 4

11th of January 2016

Jane's imaginings ended as she passed the last cottage. She looked up hopefully towards the crossroads ahead, to where she sometimes met Jack. Jack was not in her class. He was in the year above, but he always greeted Jane with a dazzling smile. She felt very safe next to his tall frame and they invariably chatted on the short journey as they walked side by side in easy comfort.

Today though, she saw no sign of him until she reached the crossroads. She stopped in disappointment at a set of footprints that marched from left to right in front of her. The footprints were larger than hers and their creator didn't seem to have hesitated at all at the junction, to see if she was coming, or wait for just a moment for her to appear. Jane recognised them instantly, and clicking her tongue in disappointment, she sighed and stepped into Jack's footprints and continued walking to school.

Taking long strides, Jane was just able to keep pace, and her progress quickened. She smiled to herself. Their footprints would spend the day together, and perhaps the next, until they melted away in beautiful sunshine. Warmed by romantic thoughts, she walked on, until interrupted by an unwelcome intruder.

Footprints smaller than Jack's, but larger than her own, exited a neat wrought iron gate that stood at the front of a neat garden and walked in step parallel to Jack's. The garden was immaculately kept and miniature conifers, laden with snow, lined the path to the front door. Light from the windows tinged the snow red, and reflected here and there, so that the conifers sparkled like Christmas trees. The house was large and double fronted, a drive at one side curved across the front and met the path at the front door. The door was framed by two ornately carved stone columns that supported a grand storm porch, and shouted the affluence of the residents to those that passed by. The gardens extended either side of the house and perfectly trimmed bushes and shrubs were carefully placed in deliberate randomness.

Another pupil at Jane's school lived there and had obviously set off ahead of Jane that morning. Despite the beauty of the scene, Jane felt a rush of jealousy that turned her view inwards and dulled her appreciation of the picture postcard garden.

"Ginny!" she hissed with a furrowed brow, and curled lip, in a manner she would not dare to Ginny's face. She spoke the name like a curse, hurling it into the cold morning where it hung in a cloud of breath, sullying the clear air.

Ginny, although only two months older than Jane, was in the school year above, she was in Jack's class, and like a stone in her shoe, was a constant irritation to Jane. Their parents were friends, consequently Jane and Ginny had known each other all their lives. They had been friends as well once and were well matched, however as they grew, a rivalry developed that was healthy at first but became toxic and consuming in time.

The change in their relationship began when Jack had

started to grow from good looking boy to handsome young man. Jane and Ginny had been drawn to him and now they competed for his attention. It grated on Jane that Ginny could spend every morning and afternoon of every school day in Jack's company. Her imagination taunted her, revealing endless possibilities of what might happen in their class. Jane knew the two of them were close, but how close? Her imagination filled the gaps in her knowledge. It provided images of Jack and Ginny sat together, their heads tilted inwards, as they talked and worked at their desks. It showed their feet touching unseen under their desks, and their forearms brushing against each other by accident or design.

Jane stood for a moment on the snow-covered path, her earlier good mood completely gone, and wondered despondently if the footprints were evidence of a grand betrayal. Had Jack and Ginny walked to school together? She pictured it in her mind.

'Yes Jack, no Jack,' Ginny would fawn and laugh too loudly at Jack's jokes–she always seemed to laugh too loudly at Jack's jokes.

Jane pondered her next course of action, and tried to decide whether to be aloof and rise above this intrusion, or spiteful and seek revenge. She tried to decide if she should continue walking in Jack's footprints and suffer Ginny's recent presence in silence? Or, if she should scuff over Ginny's footprints, and wipe them from existence? Or perhaps, if she should walk alongside Jack's footprints on the opposite side to Ginny's, then everyone that passed that way later might consider that Jane, not Ginny, had walked with Jack.

After some deliberation she decided to continue to walk in Jack's footprints and drag her schoolbag alongside across Ginny's footprints. In this way, and with some satisfaction, she soon found herself at the school gates.

The snow had been cleared in an uneven path across the playground, at the end of the cleared path stood the school, with its large doors closed to keep out the cold. It was an old Victorian school, built for fewer pupils than attended it now, its facade was dark grey and weathered, and its windows small. Behind the school, invisible from the front, two modern, brightly coloured wings had been built, with vast windows through which sunlight flooded. They contrasted the original forbidding Victorian building in glorious triumph, and provided a modern open area that Jane loved. She hurried across the playground, into the imposing building, passing under a large white banner pulled tight overhead that declared in bold red letters, '100 years of shame.'

Once inside, Jane pulled back her fur lined hood and stamped her feet on the welcome mat, creating two dusty white outlines of her walking boots. She was not the first to arrive, other children were dotted about, but they were too engrossed to acknowledge the stamping of Jane's feet or the blast of cold air through the doorway. Jane quickly unbuttoned her coat, to let the warmth in, and looked eagerly at the tables that lined the length of the corridor. It was a long corridor with a high ceiling and there were covered tables laid out on either side. On each table were plates, bowls and trays of different shape, size and colour.

Each had been lovingly piled high with delicious homemade foodstuffs.

There were sandwiches, scones and cakes on tiered cake stands, jam tarts arranged like traffic lights on trays, and mini Victoria sponge cakes that were piled high like a pyramid. Plastic containers were dotted about, full to the brim with flapjacks, Eccles cakes, cookies and biscuits. The variety of shapes and sizes of containers and foodstuffs on display gave some clue as to their origin. The majority had been carefully made in the homes of parents, grandparents and teachers. This was not a factory manufactured feast. It was homemade and lovingly created, by the townsfolk of Middle Gratestone.

Jane breathed in deeply and savoured the aroma. The smell of baking filled the corridor and beckoned invitingly. She took out an empty sandwich box and lined the bottom with cheese and cucumber sandwiches, then carefully placed on top of the sandwiches, a strawberry tart and a slice of apple pie. The slice of apple pie was of great importance and she took care in its selection, discounting many other apple pies before choosing this one.

Satisfied with her haul, Jane pressed the lid firmly onto her now full sandwich box and tucked it back into her schoolbag. With a happy spring in her step she turned and walked down the corridor to her classroom, her long black hair now released from the confines of the fur lined hood tumbled over her shoulders and bounced as she walked.

She paused on the way, next to Colin Moles–one of her classmates–who was stood next to an enormous pile of jam and cream scones. He appeared confused, and as Jane watched he looked from his overfilled sandwich box, up to the jam scone mountain in front of him, and then back to his sandwich box.

"You won't get the lid on," Jane informed him. Colin looked at Jane, looked down at his sandwich box, and then rather forlornly back up at the jam scone mountain.

"I know," he sighed but continued to stare hopefully anyway. Then in a moment of inspiration, he took two scones from his sandwich box and crammed them into his mouth before smugly squeezing the lid on. Some of the cream from the scones squeezed out of the side of the sandwich box, so he licked it off with a crumby tongue, and put the box in his bag. A neat solution to a tricky problem, he thought, and looked to see if Jane had noticed his brilliance, but she was already striding away. His full mouth prevented him calling out to announce his triumph and so reluctantly, he kept his success to himself.

Jane left the corridor, quietening the sound of arriving children excitedly helping themselves to the delights on offer, and climbed the stairs to her classroom. Mr Spinner was waiting inside.

"Good morning Jane," he said in polite welcome, a smile cracking his normally stern, pointy features. "Can I take your coat?" he enquired. Jane shrugged off the coat into Mr Spinner's bony hands and he hung it on her peg. This was not normal behaviour for her teacher. Mr Spinner was a polite and generally pleasant man, but he believed very strongly in classroom discipline and maintained a strict teacher-pupil divide. At the start of the school year, he had told Jane and her classmates that he would not tolerate overfamiliarity and they should not expect him to become their friend. However, in return for their respect and good behaviour, he would put every ounce of effort that he had into teaching them to the very highest standard. Jane enjoyed school and was very keen to learn, consequently she had heeded Mr Spinner's request and she and Mr Spinner had got on just fine.

Today though, he appeared to be quite deliberately breaking his own rules. Jane went to pull out her chair but was beaten to it by her teacher.

"Please allow me Jane," Mr Spinner offered and politely pulled out Jane's chair. "Can I get you a glass of water or anything else Jane?" Mr Spinner continued his polite onslaught.

"No thank you Mr Spinner," Jane declined in defence. Mr Spinner beamed at her and then moved to the classroom door to await the next arrival. He slavishly followed the same routine with all the children, as if under orders to do so, until the whole class was present and seated in silence at their desks. After ticking off the register, he announced very politely, with a broad smile, that the class were to move quietly to the school hall for assembly.

Chapter 5

11th of January 1916

Dawn arrived and brought with it bitter pain in Alfred's joints. He had slept cross-legged, hunched over with his head in his hands. His fingers were numb with cold and he shook uncontrollably. Wisps of smoke came from the charred remains of the fire that had recently lost its fight for life, and fresh snow lay everywhere in the clearing except on the blackened smoking circle. The fox was gone and there were no prints in the snow to mark its presence.

Alfred stood slowly and started to swing his arms and stamp his feet to get the blood flowing to his cold extremities, he coughed light clouds of fog as the freezing air irritated his lungs. The sky had lightened to blue, chasing the dark away and had left behind terrible cold and beautiful crisp white snow. He listened to the sound of the wood for a while and then cursed himself. He should have used the cover of darkness to raid the cottages on Church Road and plunder food for his breakfast. Sleep had seduced him and now he faced an uncertain day with only hunger for company.

Needing warmth, Alfred set about reviving the fire. First, he removed the paper from the seat of his thin cotton trousers and tore off another strip. Then sitting back down, he tore it into smaller pieces and placed them in the smoking embers of the fire, there they caught alight, curled and blackened. Quickly Alfred used more kindling and built the fire back up, he might have to face the day hungry, but he did not have to face it cold and hungry.

Feeling under the tree trunk with his numb fingers, he found and retrieved the cake tin, from which he took out a smaller tin then replaced the cake tin back in its hiding place. The smaller tin had a handle fashioned from some steel wire and fed through two holes at the top of the tin. He filled the tin with snow then used the handle to suspend the tin over the fire. Once the snow in the tin had melted, Alfred placed it on the ground to allow the tin to cool, so that he wouldn't burn his lips on it, and then drank greedily. He repeated the process until at last he felt full and refreshed.

"Right then," he said quietly to himself. "Let's see what this day has to offer." After one final listen to the sounds of the woodland, he made sure everything was packed away, put out the fire, and left the security of the hideout.

It didn't feel like early morning anymore, the sun was visible through the trees, though Alfred felt no heat from it on his face. It was bitterly cold away from the fire and the snow clung unthawed to the leafless tree branches. The snow on the ground quietened the sound of the leaves rustling underfoot as Alfred passed and he made his way along the animal tracks in near silence. Slowly, he drew to the edge of the woods and looked out. The dirty, moss covered roof of the church across the road, had been replaced with white icing that shone brilliantly in the sunshine. The road had a pristine covering of snow and only the path alongside had a small number of footprints to tell the tale of those that had braved the morning. Alfred held his breath, watching and listening as he did so for any signs of life. A robin landed on a tree branch not far from him, looked at him for a moment, puffed out its red breast then flew off again, all seemed quiet and calm.

He looked towards the poorhouse and wondered how his brother was. Had he slept okay without Alfred? Had he been warm in the night? Alfred felt a pang of guilt that he was not there to look after him but then reassured himself.

"Better in there than out here freezing." A winter like this was no place for his little brother. Perhaps Alfred would go to him in the spring. They could run away together and enjoy the warmer months in the freedom of the countryside. Alfred liked that thought and dallied for a moment as he enjoyed it. They could eat rabbit and venison, Alfred had trapped them before and he was accurate with a sling and shot. They could cook on a camp fire and eat the succulent meat together. Alfred salivated at the thought and suddenly his hunger returned, dispelling his daydream, and he was back in the woods lying in the snow.

It was time to find food so without further hesitation he stood up, sprang out into the open, careful not to leave tell-tale tracks, and stepped in to one of the sets of tracks already made on the path. Smoke was drifting idly from the cottage chimneys on Church Road, Alfred passed them and the poorhouse next to the church, unaware again that unfriendly eyes were watching his every move.

He spent the day outside, walking from one place to the next, looking for food. His sturdy boots and two sets of socks kept his feet warm and dry but the cold cut through the cotton night shirt, and his own shirt, so much that he felt his bones were freezing. A deep ache grew in them as the cold bit deeper and deeper, and soon it pained him to walk. He kept his hands clenched in the woollen sock-gloves and wedged them into his armpits to keep them warm. The moment he exposed his fingers to the bitter air they hurt and felt cold and useless. He pulled the oversize flat cap down over his ears and walked stubbornly on.

Alfred found no help that day. The markets were closed, the butchers, the bakers and the grocers, all had their produce indoors, the tables outside kept bare to avoid anything freezing. The farmers' fields were frozen and snow covered. However, the wooden fences that partitioned them were broken in places and allowed Alfred easy access, so he scratched around in the fields, uncovering large areas of rock hard ground underneath the snow. He worked doggedly, with a piece of wood he had prised from the fence, blistering his cold hands and catching splinters in the process. The effort should have warmed his muscles but the wind whipped across the open fields and took his strength and energy with it.

The ground resisted all his attempts to dig down deep, to where he might find some root vegetables that he could boil over his fire. As the day started to close and the sun dipped towards the horizon, the shadows grew longer and colder, and Alfred had to admit defeat. Desperation began to get the better of him so he decided to try his luck inside the shops. He headed for the bakery.

With a deep breath, and a mutter of encouragement to himself, he opened the bakery door. A small bell, positioned just above his head, angrily announced his entrance.

"Just a minute," a gruff voice shouted from the backroom. There was no one at the shop counter. Alfred propped the door open with a heavy stone that had been carved into the shape of a loaf, it obviously served as a doorstop in warmer months, and quietly as he could, stepped forward. He silently reached over the counter and grabbed a large loaf sat on paper ready to be wrapped at the counter.

"I know who you are boy." A man in an apron had appeared in the open doorway behind the counter. Alfred had come here many times with his mother and recognised the owner of the bakery.

"Please Mr Rose," Alfred had tears in his eyes. "I'm desperate," Alfred kept his hand on the loaf and didn't move. He could easily grab it and be out of the open door before the baker could get under the counter. Mr Rose was old, and even though Alfred was weak from hunger and the cold, he felt certain he could run the faster of the two.

They eyed each other like prize fighters, each waiting for the other to make a move. Alfred understood that he needed the goodwill of the town to stay alive and well, if he stole this loaf today, the word would go out and everyone would be after him. He needed to convince Mr Rose to give him the loaf of bread. Mr Rose's eyes hardened.

"There's a war on, you don't steal when there's a war on, now put it down and out you go," he didn't sound like he would change his mind.

"I need it," pleaded Alfred. He could smell the freshly baked bread and feel the crust crunch under his fingers.

"We all need it. I need it," said Mr Rose venomously.

He shifted his weight, and for the first time, Alfred noticed the heavy wooden rolling pin in the baker's hands, the knuckles were white, and Alfred realised his chances of getting away were less than he first thought. Slowly he let go of the loaf and moved away back towards the door.

"Shut it on your way out," said Mr Rose. Alfred left the warmth of the bakery and walked quickly away in the icy cold.

His brief stay inside had done nothing to warm the cold set deep in his bones. He was anxious now and shaken from his confrontation with the baker.

"He could have let me have it," he said to himself. "Father fixed his roof," he recalled from two summers ago. "He could have let me have it," Alfred turned and stared back at the row of shops. "I hate you!" he screamed. "I hate you all," he turned and in a stumbling exhausted run, made his way back towards Church Road. He desperately needed to warm himself by the fire and melt snow to drink. The cold was so deep inside him he thought that he was already frozen. Perhaps tonight he could raid the cottages on Church Road and pick up some tasty morsels left over from supper. He clung to that thought and hurried along in the cold approaching evening.

Alfred was somewhat surprised to arrive back at the wood. His mind had started to drift and he found it increasingly difficult to concentrate. He had failed to observe his surroundings as he walked and was now slightly confused to be here so soon. His anger had kept him going and he had seethed at everyone he could think of as he staggered along. Now the desire to warm himself by the fire consumed him, his situation was desperate, and he knew it.

He rushed straight into the woods, without checking if he was being observed and not caring about leaving tracks in the snow. The temperature was dropping as the sun disappeared below the horizon, it was colder still under the canopy of trees where shade had defied the winter sun. Alfred stumbled and crawled to the centre of the woodland and the safety of the clearing. The animal tracks seemed more confusing now and it was some time before he reached the hideout.

As he entered the clearing he stopped. Something was wrong. The hairs on the back of his neck stood up as his confused mind tried to make sense of what he was seeing.

"Footprints," he muttered. "There are too many." As well as Alfred's footprints that led directly away from the root end of the tree and into the woods, there was at least one other set. The feet were about the same size as Alfred's and walked this way and that in exploration. Alfred looked to the entrance of his hideout and with a sinking heart saw that in addition to his tracks there was another set that led both in and out of the gap between the two trees. Whoever had been there had discovered the hideout, and left.

Alfred slowly pulled back the brush that covered the entrance and peered inside. He was nervous and hoped that he was perhaps mistaken and that his refuge remained undiscovered. The snow that lay inside had been trampled down by the intruder as they had searched the interior, and the kindling had been kicked around and stamped into the snow, rendering it useless.

Alfred walked in, knelt, and reached under the tree

trunk for the cake tin. Not immediately finding it he shuffled along and reached again. Panicking now he raked his hand up and down the crevice catching his knuckles and drawing blood, the sudden pain stopped him and with dread he realised the cake tin had been discovered and removed by the intruder. A feeling of utter desolation and loneliness came over Alfred and he looked up at the darkening sky and wept. He was shaking again, his hands were wet and cold from crawling, lumps of snow clung to the socks he had fashioned as gloves, and he clenched his hands in pain.

"Please help me," he said to the sky, through teary eyes. "Please," he sobbed as desperation took over. The pain and anguish came out of him in great sobs that took his breath away, he gasped for air in between sobs and retreated into himself. He stayed like that for a while, as the sun set and light left the woodland, he stayed until he could cry no more and the shaking from the cold had stopped.

Finally, realising he had to do something, he looked down at his hands, his fingers inside the snow encrusted socks were clawed in the half light. He looked around. The snow, where it lay, gave a false light to the clearing, the rest of the wood was dark, unforgiving and cold.

Alfred crawled out of his hideout, away from the clearing, along the animal tracks. He closed his eyes in the darkness, to prevent them being stabbed by an unseen twig or thorn, and felt his way with numb hands. His face became scratched by sharp brambles and thorns, and he continually bumped his head as he pushed on blindly unaware of his direction. The animal tracks twisted and turned through the woods and Alfred was soon lost in the darkness. He tried to steer a path that was roughly straight, but without light to provide a landmark, and with trees and brambles barring his way and causing him to change direction, he became disorientated. His mind wandered and he thought of his mother cooking dinner at the stove while he and his brothers basked in its warmth.

'Dinner's ready,' she called them to the table kindly. 'Grace please Alfred,' she would say to Father before they could eat. Alfred became oblivious to his predicament, and smiled in the darkness at an image of his older brother trying to sneak a morsel of food from the table while everyone else's eyes were shut. His brother received a rap on the knuckles from Mother for his efforts.

'Ouch,' he had cried out in the middle of Father's grace.

Alfred touched his head and realised he had banged it very hard on something unforgiving and with some surprise realised it was he that had exclaimed out loud in pain. He was still on his hands and knees and tried to push himself upright to survey his surroundings. However, the feeling in his hands had gone and his arms felt rooted in the snow. His strength was failing and he was unable to raise himself away from the hard, icy ground. Alfred leant forward and placed the side of his head against the hard object in front of him. It was rough and scratched at his cheek.

He opened his eyes and looked up, it was lighter here outside of the tree canopy and Alfred realised he had made it to the side of the cottages on Church Road. On the other side of the road stood the church, planted in the snow, there was light coming from the windows and like a moth

Alfred was drawn towards it.

He crawled slowly across the road, his hands and knees were bleeding now, and he smeared specks of blood in the snow. They looked black where they smudged in the shadow but were bright crimson red in the light from the church. The stained-glass window in the church, emblazoned an image of an angel with wings and carrying a harp, on the ground. It lit a colourful path for Alfred to follow. He crawled forward, as he did so, his tracks disrupted the image in the snow. He left a corrupted and disfigured angel behind him as if his passing had robbed it of beauty.

Finally, he made it to the gate and crawled down the path towards the large oak doors that stood tall and forbidding at the end. The door was iron bound and a large iron knocker was placed high at head height. Alfred looked up. He would not be able to reach it from his hands and knees. So, using a gravestone as a prop, and summoning the last of his failing strength, he pulled himself unsteadily to his feet. The door was only a few short steps away but Alfred feared he would fall before he could reach it. It might as well have been a mile, but gritting his teeth, he held onto the gravestone and reached out with his other hand. As he stretched toward it and prepared to take a step, certain he would fall, the door opened.

Light flooded out and the shadow of the vicar, dark and unwelcoming, stretched down the path to the gate. He saw Alfred straight away, caught in the light from the doorway.

"Please," pleaded Alfred in a quiet, low voice, bereft of strength. "Please can I come in and warm myself, I may die out here it's too cold." The vicar looked at him for a moment.

"Young Alfred," the vicar sighed. There was pity in his voice, but the slight shake of his head made Alfred think the vicar had rather he had not seen him at all. He sounded resigned as if he had no choice in what he was about to say. "What a sorry soul you are," the vicar continued. "You stand here before the Lord's house, begging for help, after you have stolen from the poorhouse. You stole clothes left for the children that I see you are wearing now in contempt of this town's kindness. You stole food from the poorhouse pantry. You even tried to steal bread from the bakery. Yes, I know about that. And now you stand here before me, unrepentant. I have no doubt that you are here to steal from the church. What will it be? Money from the collection? Food from my own larder? No Alfred, I will not let you in so that you may pillage the church and condemn your soul to purgatory." The vicar finished in a shout as if stood in the church pulpit, delivering a fiery sermon to his congregation, and looked at Alfred.

"Please Sir," said Alfred. "Please help me." The vicar saw the desperation in Alfred's eyes.

"I have business to attend to," the vicar replied harshly. "For your own good I will not allow you in the church on your own. Wait here and when I return, you can warm yourself inside. I have food and water, you can have your fill and we will decide what to do with you tomorrow. Do not expect leniency."

Alfred nodded, and the vicar turned and locked the door with a large key tied at his waist. He pocketed the key and walked past Alfred without another word, leaving Alfred leaning unsteadily on the gravestone. Alfred watched the vicar walk up the road into town, and continued to watch long after the road was deserted, hoping that the vicar would have a change of heart and come back and let him in.

He tried to work out when the vicar would return. How long will he be gone? What business is he on? Alfred stood in the snow and watched the road until he lost all hope. He felt so alone, he was scared, and he didn't have the strength left to try to go somewhere else.

"I've been watching you," a voice said from behind him. Alfred couldn't turn, his hand was frozen to the gravestone and it took everything he had left to remain standing. He recognised the voice though. It was Henry, the policeman's son, a boy of Alfred's age. They had gone to school together and had often fought. Henry was a bully and picked on the smaller children in the school. He had tripped up Alfred's little brother once and laughed when little Alfred cried. Alfred saw it happen, and beat Henry with his fists, until Henry's nose and lips bled. Henry hated Alfred but until now that hadn't mattered to Alfred at all.

"I think you've lost something," said Henry as he circled around Alfred. He stopped in front of him and Alfred saw he had the cake tin under his arm. Henry was dressed in a greatcoat that hung almost to his boots. He had a hat, scarf and gloves, and looked warm and rosy cheeked. "Cold tonight isn't it," Henry said, looking Alfred up and down–appraising him. "The vicar won't be back for a while; they've got a town meeting see, about how to look after the old and the poor during this cold weather." Henry smiled and then laughed. “Funny that seeing as he left you here on his doorstep.” He laughed again, a deep malicious laugh that lasted too long. “I’ve got something for you!” Henry exclaimed in mock surprise. “I almost forgot, anyway here we are.” He opened the cake tin. “Here’s a photo of your family,” he held it up to Alfred just out of his reach so that Alfred could see the picture.

It was the last one that had been taken of them all together. His mother had insisted they get it done prior to Father going off to war. Alfred remembered the day well, they had all bathed and had their hair cut and combed prior to visiting the photographer. It had rained though and they had danced around puddles and ran from cover to cover to get there. His mother fussed over them all morning but then laughed as they dodged the rain. By the time they got to the photography shop they were all soaked.

“No? You don’t want it? Okay.” Henry dropped the photo in the snow at Alfred’s feet as if it was just rubbish. “What about this flint? It looks useful. You could light a lovely fire with this.” Alfred looked at the flint in Henry’s hand. “No? You don’t want this either?” Henry closed his hand over the flint, span on his foot, and flung it as far as he could into the night. “You can get that back when the snow thaws,” he laughed. “You know what,” Henry continued. I quite like this cake tin I’m sure I could find a use for it.”

Turning it upside down, Henry emptied the last of the contents into the snow and replaced the lid. Alfred looked at the remnants of his life, lying in the snow, far out of reach. He could see the telegrams that brought the news of the death of his father and brother and letters that they had sent from the front that always cheerily avoided any mention of danger.

"Cheerio then," Henry said and turned to leave. "Oh, hang on, there's one more thing," Henry turned back suddenly and punched Alfred on the nose. It was clumsy and unpractised, and ordinarily Alfred would have easily brushed it aside, but tonight he was exhausted and his limbs frozen. He saw it coming but was unable to force himself to move in time. Pain exploded in Alfred's head and unable to find the strength to stand, he fell to the floor, crashing down on his side in the snow.

He heard Henry's footsteps crunching away and soon all was quiet. The pain quickly receded as Alfred lay there. He couldn't quite see the church door anymore because he was lying just off the path behind a gravestone. I must shout to the vicar when he comes back, thought Alfred, determined to keep his eyes open. He will have to carry me now, he smiled to himself.

His mind drifted as he lay in the snow and started to play tricks on him. He saw the vicar, the policeman and the mayor in front of him in the snow. They were sat at a table having a town council meeting, they laughed with the other important townsfolk that were also there and drank warm ale in front of the fire at the inn.

He saw his little brother thrown out of the poorhouse into the snow by George Edmund, who laughed manically as he did so. The town councillors pointed and laughed at Alfred's brother crying, cold and alone in the snow.

He saw the baker, stuffing so much bread into his mouth that his hysterical laughing was muffled, and crumbs and hunks of bread fell on the ground, where they were trampled until inedible by Henry. The councillors and George Edmund all laughed and pointed at the baker coughing out bread and Henry stamping around in the snow.

Alfred hated them all, his hatred burned inside him like a furnace, it melted the snow around him and it steamed and fizzled in the night. Alfred pushed himself to his knees, hate had brought his strength back and it scorched the ground. As he looked he saw Death approaching, tall and dark, and carrying a scythe, just as Alfred had once seen in a book. Death walked around the councillor's table and slowly beckoned Alfred with a skeletal hand. Alfred opened out his arms.

"I'm ready," he said clearly. Death beckoned again and turned, without hesitation Alfred stood up and followed into the night, away from the mocking laughter.

The town councillors had indeed had a meeting that night. It lasted until the early hours as they usually did when they were held at the inn. They discussed how to look after the poor, and the elderly, and many decisions were made as Alfred's body froze in the night. Alfred's name was not mentioned, not even by the vicar. It snowed again during the meeting, and Alfred's body, lying outside the church just behind a gravestone, lay undiscovered until Sunday morning four days later. It thawed that morning and he was found as people gathered for Sunday service.

It was a particularly embarrassing public occasion on which to find a boy's body in the snow. The people of Middle Gratestone were outraged. A public hearing was held and those involved in Alfred's death were forced to tell of their part.

The town charter was rewritten in response, to prevent such evil neglect ever happening again, and trust funds were created to support the town's children for years to come. None of this helped Alfred though, and he was buried with his family in the church graveyard, the whole town attended his funeral and prayed for the salvation of his soul and for their own.

Chapter 6

"Good morning children and welcome to school today on this very special one-hundred-year centenary of shame day." The headmaster stood on the stage with his arms wide and boomed out his greeting, his large jowls wobbled and his belly bounced in time to his words. The stage was at one end of the large assembly hall in the oldest part of the school. The ceiling in the hall was high and the walls were covered in polished wood panelling, shined to perfection by the school cleaners.

Above the stage, mounted on the wall, were several large wooden boards that listed the previous head boys and head girls that had attended the school in years gone by. Their names were engraved on brass plaques mounted on the boards, and dared those pupils that followed to match their achievement. Ginny's name was the latest addition. Her brass plaque gleamed brightly in pride of place behind the headmaster.

He stood next to a grand lectern, planted in the middle of the stage. The school crest was painted on the front of it, although the paint was old and faded as if it had been applied centuries ago.

He always stood next to the lectern and never behind it, Jane had observed. He was the only teacher to do this, every other teacher when they had cause to take the stage, stood directly behind it, even Miss Brown who was so short just the top of her head was visible.

In contrast, the headmaster was a large man, well known for his ability to speak constantly in a loud cheerful voice that could be heard from great distance. Consequently, as he could be heard approaching from such a long way off, it was very rare that he caught any children breaking his school rules. He would walk the corridors and be greeted in chorus by children, warned of his imminent arrival, that all appeared to be behaving impeccably. Now, in the assembly hall, his voice carried to every corner of the room.

"I hope you have all helped yourselves to the delightful food laid out in the entrance hall this morning. This has been provided by the local community, particularly, your teachers and parents, so I would like to take this opportunity to pass on my thanks to them all for their time and kind generosity," the headmaster clapped to the teachers that were dotted around the room.

"However, this is not a celebration," he said firmly with one finger raised, his face changing abruptly to one that was sterner. "No, it is not. It is an anniversary of the most shameful day in our town's history, a day when the townsfolk of Middle Gratestone stood by and did nothing. A day when we allowed the unthinkable, the unforgivable, to happen, a day that must never be forgotten lest we deny our guilt. Because today it is the anniversary of the day one hundred years ago upon which to our eternal shame we let a child die." He paused for effect and looked around at the young faces before him. He had their absolute attention. There was no whispering or fidgeting. All the children were rock still and looked up attentively. He continued his welcome speech in a lower pitched tone his expression grave and serious.

"As a result of our shame the town leaders met and wrote down in town law that we would never ever neglect a child again. For one hundred years since that day we have kept the children of this town safe." The headmaster clapped his hands in applause and the children and teachers assembled followed suit. After a few seconds the headmaster stopped clapping and everyone else immediately stopped as well.

"The town set up the school trust, the sports trust, the orphan trust and the town watch trust." The headmaster paused again as if marking a full stop and then continued. "So that we adults do not forget that we let you children down so shamefully, one hundred years ago, we always commemorate the anniversary of shame day every year. A day on which children will want for nothing, a day on which all adults make sure that all children have the best day ever, a day on which we remind ourselves that children are the most important things in our town, and in our lives, and in our world." The headmaster looked around the assembly hall.

"The children!" he shouted.

"The children!" all the other teachers and staff shouted back. The headmaster paused and allowed the room to quieten.

"Of course, on this day we must also remember the boy Alfred. A boy known to many of you as, the shame of Middle Gratestone, he is the boy that we let down all those years ago, and we must never forget him. I would now like to invite our head girl, Ginny, to the stage to read Alfred's story as recorded in the town charter, the story of, the shame of Middle Gratestone." The headmaster's voice slowly got quieter, he wiped an imaginary tear from the corner of his eye and then started to applaud.

Everyone clapped as Ginny came to the stage, although Jane unconsciously and imperceptibly clapped a little slower. Ginny walked purposefully and reached the lectern on the stage before the applause stopped. She stood tall and proud, her blonde hair, drawn back in a ponytail, revealed her clear skin and delicate features. She was dressed in a matching skirt and business jacket with a white revere shirt underneath. Sixth formers were not required to wear school uniform, another point of irritation for Jane, who was only narrowly too young for the senior year. Most of the other sixth formers, including Jack, were dressed casually, however Ginny had obviously dressed to make an impact today. In appearance and manner, she was the model student and she smiled radiantly to her audience. With a sweet clear voice, without a hint of a nervous tremor, she began to read.

"The shame of Middle Gratestone, an account of the happenings of the 10th and 11th of January 1916, written by James Petherbridge, Town Mayor," Ginny looked up. "My Great, Great Grandfather," she said to those assembled, although all her schoolmates already knew this fact because she had told them so on many occasions.

Jane raised her eyebrows at those sat next to her on small wooden chairs and looked to the heavens in fake exasperation. She caught Jack's eye and he smiled at her through a throng of heads, Jane smiled back and looked around to see if anyone had seen this secret exchange, their first of the day, and then looked down. Her cheeks reddened, and unknown to her, made Jack think she looked even more beautiful and he held his stare long after Jane had broken hers.

Jack often found himself staring at Jane. He was in the enviable position of being the object of affection of the two best looking girls in school and was torn between the two like a child with a choice of ice-cream or sweets.

Ginny had long blonde hair, she was tall, graceful and she stood out in a crowd like a blonde beacon. She engaged people with a natural charm and could always be found at the centre of a group of children all baying for her attention. She was the Omega female and presided over her schoolmates like a matriarch.

Jane was dark haired and green eyed, she was much more mysterious and maintained a cool demeanour. Her sharp wit was legendary amongst her schoolmates and her eyes so green that most boys found themselves clumsy and dim witted in her presence. Jack often tried to break through Jane's defence, but she never opened up and invariably they talked without saying anything at all.

Ginny's voice eroded the moment of mutual agreeable pleasure and Jack and Jane started to pay attention. It was a story that all the children had heard before, told often in the words of the town mayor from the record in the town charter, but pictured now in fine detail in their minds. They settled quietly and imagined what it must have been like to be the boy Alfred all those years ago. Ginny's voice kept their imaginations in time, they all saw the same horrible scene, and all thought the same thoughts. All fearfully pictured the same horror that happened in their town, to a child just like them, one hundred years ago, they listened and brought the story to life in their minds.

Chapter 7

Later that morning, at the church on Church Road, Jane waited with her classmates to enter the church grounds. The marshmallow snow drifts that had earlier softened the harsh corners and straight lines of the town, were being trampled down by milling feet. The path into the church graveyard was choked with children, slowly moving through the break in the low, snow covered wall. A cold cloud from their breathing and chatting, hung in the air just overhead and drifted slowly in the light wind like a sea fog. An occasional snow ball was secretly hoisted into the air from out of the mist, despite cautions and strong words from teachers trying to maintain control over the wilful crowd.

One of Jane's classmates was receiving a stern talking to from Mr Spinner. Moments earlier, he had been slowly circling Mr Spinner while Jane watched in interest. He had been caught though and now had to take the lengthy questioning about what he thought he had been doing. He glanced sheepishly at Jane, who smiled back broadly from behind Mr Spinner, just out of the teacher's eye line. She made an 'L' sign with the forefinger and thumb of her right hand and put it up to her forehead.

"Loser," she mouthed. The boy tried to stifle a half smile, but Mr Spinner spotted it and increased the volume of his irate questioning.

Jane moved away, down the path a little, and hopped over the wall near to where the headmaster stood in the graveyard, next to four old graves. Children were starting to gather in the area in loose formation, ushered by their teachers. Jane looked at the four gravestones, two of them were outwardly very similar they were originally white and they carried the same inscription. The words were weathered by wind and rain but still clear. 'Greater love hath no man than this that lays down his life for his friends. John 15:13.' One of the two was also inscribed 'Alfred, loving husband and father' the other was inscribed 'Alfred, loving son and brother.'

The third gravestone was less grand and had weathered terribly. Crumbs of stone that had lost the fight against the wind and rain, peppered the ground around its base. Time had dabbed on lichen in splotches of greens, yellows and blues that coloured the grey stone in a mosaic of fauna. The letters carved in the stone were blurred and indistinct despite it carrying the same year as the first two, 1915. Perhaps this gravestone had been erected on a smaller budget, Jane thought.

She struggled to read the inscription but finally could make it out, it was inscribed 'Edith, wife and mother, died of a broken heart.' Jane wondered for a moment how much pain and sorrow it must take for someone to die of a broken heart and what could cause such a thing to happen. She felt incredibly sad as she imagined what it must have felt like. Poor woman, she thought.

The fourth grave was slightly shorter than the others, but the headstone was the grandest of them all. It was fully a foot taller than the other three and was made from beautiful white marble that had recently been cleaned. The inscription read 'Here lies Alfred, died alone and in torment, to the eternal shame of the people of Middle

Gratestone.' It was dated the 11th of January 1916, exactly 100 years previous.

The headmaster saw Jane reading the inscriptions. Jane was a clever girl and always attentive in class, he enjoyed testing her keen mind and took every opportunity to pass on his wisdom and knowledge.

"He was the first person from the town to go to the Great War you know," he informed Jane, and she looked up in response. "Alfred senior," the headmaster clarified, pointing to the gravestone that was inscribed 'Alfred, loving husband and father.' "The first from Middle Gratestone to fight in the First World War, his eldest son followed him as soon as he was old enough," he said, pointing to the gravestone that was inscribed 'Alfred, loving son and brother.' "They died together in France on the same day, in the same battle–all that rushing to get killed..." the headmaster was lost in thought for a moment then continued.

"Nobody knows who died first but they were found together, side by side, and were brought home together, side by side. Now here they lay. I wonder did Alfred senior see his son killed or did Alfred junior see his father killed? I don't know how it happened, but they were found together, and they have been together ever since. Anyway, thinking about how it had happened, and who went first, tore Edith apart," the headmaster moved a step closer to the worn weathered gravestone that Jane had struggled to read. "And her heart just gave out. That left the two younger boys parentless. The one you see lying here," he pointed to the grand marble gravestone. "And another lost to the poorhouse. The two younger boys were both called Alfred as well. Edith was partial to the name. It was her father's name and when she married an Alfred she thought it was a lucky sign and insisted all their children were called Alfred as well. Very fortunate they didn't have a girl." The headmaster smiled and winked at Jane before continuing. "Lord only knows how confusing it was for them all in their house. They lived in a worker's cottage just here on Church Road, but once Edith died, the paper factory put the young boys in the poorhouse and moved a new worker in. They were 'worker's cottages' they said and the boys weren't workers." The headmaster shook his head in disbelief. "That was the start of it, and this was the end of it," he pointed to the graves in front of him and then looked up. "Ah we're all here."

"Children!" he boomed so loudly that two crows standing sentinel on a church gargoyle, took flight and angrily cawed their displeasure in return. The headmaster looked at the crows, and paused to allow distance to quieten their raucous cries. "Children," he said quietly, confident that everyone was now listening. "I have gathered you here today to say a prayer for the shame of Middle Gratestone, and in memory of the boy Alfred. It is a tragedy that a child can die, and beyond understanding that he can die parentless and unloved. Please bow your heads in respect."

The headmaster waited for the children to settle and then began to recite from memory. "Please God we pray to you, be a father to Alfred. You are his mind with which to think. Give him guidance and advice as he grows in heaven, and provide him a strong arm to hold when he is tired. Be his rock and example, so that he may grow in Teach him strength so that he may have compassion, fo is your son. Please God we pray to you, be a mother to Alfred. You are his heart with which to love. Teach him love and gentleness, kindness and trust, so that he can love in his turn. Hold him when he is hurt and let him run when he is not, for he is your son. Please God we pray to you, be a brother to Alfred. You are his right arm which makes him strong. Run and play with him in the open fields, test him and compete with him. Fight against him, fight with him, and fight for him, for he is your brother. Please God we pray to you, be a sister to Alfred. You are his eyes to see and his ears to hear. Be reason and common sense, tell him when he is wrong and tell him when he is right. Fill his world with colour and sound so that he does not know dark and quiet, and he lives in the light. Be proud of him as he learns and grows, for he is your brother. Please God we pray to you. Be a family for Alfred. You are his legs that support him. Nurture and protect him so that he can grow tall. Help him to become all that he can be, for he is your family. Amen." The headmaster looked up at the bowed heads that were slowly lifting to reveal blinking eyes and solemn faces. "We will now have one minute of silence, please think of Alfred."

Jane bowed her head and tried to think of Alfred during happy times, perhaps playing hide and seek with his brothers while out on a family picnic. They must have had picnics one hundred years ago, they must have had hide and seek one hundred years ago. She lost her train of thought and the happy image of a family picnic was lost with rough her clothes and her toes were as she stood in the snow. Very hard to the sun on a day like today, she thought. snowball fight on Haldon hill. That's where we go to sledging when it snows maybe they went there as well.

"Thank you," the headmaster said. Jane looked up, some of her classmates had tears in their eyes and Jane felt instantly guilty that she did not. Perhaps she should have thought of sad things. More of her classmates looked bored and totally miserable in the cold though, so Jane felt a little better and looked to the headmaster to find out what was going to happen next. Back to school and lunch she hoped.

She was particularly looking forward to the apple pie. She suspected it had been made by Jack's grandmother, a lady renowned for her apple pie. Jane had had some before, Jack had brought a whole apple pie to her front door in the autumn and explained that his grandmother had made so many they couldn't freeze them all. So, would she want one? She recalled that the pastry had melted in her mouth to reveal the sharp sweet taste of apple, so incredibly succulent and juicy.

"Right then," the headmaster's voice shook Jane from her salivation. "I understand that some of you have brought gifts to leave for Alfred. I think they are best left at the statue of Alfred. There is not enough space here at the graves. So, if you would please all file past Alfred's statue, pay your respects and leave what you will, we will reassemble outside the church gate. Chop, chop I'm sure you are all cold."

Jane did not want to go anywhere near the statue of Alfred, she had never liked it, and at the end of the headmaster's words a chill ran deep down her spine and her senses became keener making the snow seem whiter and brighter, it now seemed to crunch under the children's feet much louder in Jane's ears. She was no longer cold and all thoughts of apple pie were banished from her mind. With a deliberate physical effort, she forced her head around and looked to the statue in quiet dread. It was further into the graveyard, stood slightly apart from other statues, and was mounted on a stone plinth. Jane could see its stark blackness, vivid against the other pale statues and white snow. Strange the snow had not lain on it, she thought, perhaps they had brushed it off for the ceremony? She felt a gravestone behind her knees, and belatedly realised as she toppled over that her fear had got the better of her and she had been unconsciously walking backwards away from the statue.

"Got you," Jack's voice said from behind her. She felt safe hands arrest her fall and gently push her forwards. "You look like you've seen a ghost," he remarked. Jane shook her head, the lump in her throat receded as she looked into Jack's blue eyes.

"This is the place to see one," she replied, surprising herself at how level and calm her voice sounded. A startled yell from behind them stunted their budding conversation and they both turned to see what the commotion was.

"Ouch! Something bit me," exclaimed Mr Spinner. Clearly surprised, he stepped back away from Alfred's gravestone, on which he had been resting his hand, and then instinctively sucked at the bite in the web of his thumb. Mr Spinner had been hanging back to make sure none of the children hopped over the wall to avoid paying their respects to Alfred. Now though, Jane could see he was preoccupied, and perhaps she had a chance to avoid going up to the statue. "Damn thing," swore Mr Spinner, as he prodded around in a crack in the gravestone with a twig he had quickly scavenged from the ground. "Show yourself and let me squash you," he threatened, wanting to see exactly what it was that had bitten him and at least get the satisfaction of squashing the offending creature. Jane's good nature got the better of her.

"Are you okay Mr Spinner?" she asked.

"Yes, Yes," he replied without looking at her, and continued stabbing the twig into the crack with increasing violence. "Off you go, up with the others," he dismissed her.

Jack smiled, "come on let's go up together," he said gently, briefly placing his palm in the small of Jane's back, and then shyly removing it, suddenly shocked by his own daring. Jane nodded and stepped forward, aware only of the faintest touch but emboldened by it, and headed towards the statue. She looked up, a chill ran down her spine again. As the children edged forward, and paid their respects, Jane kept her eyes firmly on the statue, looking for something to fear, ready to run if necessary.

"Have you ever touched him?" asked Jack.

"No of course not!" Jane exclaimed in shock. "Why would I? Why would anyone?" Jack looked secretive and replied quietly so that only Jane would hear.

"I have," he leant in a little closer and whispered in Jane's ear. "He's warm." Jane recoiled and looked at Jack who nodded in affirmation. "That's why the snow's melted," he pointed to the statue in proof.

Jane's eyes followed the line of Jack's finger to the statue. She felt terror and panic building up inside her, she was sure she would be sick any second and tried to swallow the lump in her throat. Her knees felt weak as if they were going to buckle and she grabbed Jack's arm for support. Why was it warm? She questioned. What was warming it up? Jack looked down at Jane's hand gripping his arm, and up at the profile of her face, her eyes were wide in fear. Realising she may continue to hold his arm if she was scared, Jack started to talk in a low slow voice.

"No one knows where the statue came from. No one built it, no one paid for it. It just appeared overnight exactly one year after Alfred died. It's said that the statue looks exactly like he did when he begged the vicar for his life. Crying without tears and too cold to walk." Jane squeezed his arm in protest.

"Stop it," she said loudly. The children in front of them turned and looked, Jane's voice was clipped in fear and they saw it in her eyes.

"You're scared," Ginny said.

"No, she's not," Jack jumped in, suddenly feeling selfish and hurtful, and regretting his words to Jane. "She's cold that's all." Jane withdrew her hand from Jack's arm and stared down her accuser.

"No," she said, idly playing with a lock of her hair that

protruded from her purple woollen beret. "I was just listening to Alfred; you know 'the shame.' I commune with him sometimes. He says he's going to eat your soul, then sick it up, and eat it again." Jack spluttered out a laugh and Ginny's eyes narrowed.

"You're disgusting... and you're scared." Ginny said but Jane ignored the remark.

"It's your turn," she pointed to Ginny. Ginny turned, nodded briefly to the statue of Alfred, and moved on.

"Now you," she shouted back at Jane, who was stranded next in line. Other children looked over, alerted by Ginny's shout, and started to watch. Jane remained stranded the wrong side of the statue.

"It'll be okay," Jack said under his breath so that only Jane could hear. Jane looked at the children that were staring at her in anticipation. She stepped forward keeping her eyes on Ginny so as not to have to look at the statue.

"Touch it," said Ginny, capitalising on Jane's fear. Jane felt the fear bubbling up inside her again. She wanted to run, she wanted to scream 'no' and keep running until she was home. She wanted her mum to hold her and tell her everything was okay. "Touch it," Ginny said again firmly, her mouth set in a thin line and her fists clenched at her side.

Time seemed to stop for Jane, she felt she was floating somewhere outside her body. There was no sound that she could hear. There was no wind or cold that she could feel. There was just terror boiling inside her. She looked into Ginny's eyes and saw that the contempt that she could always see there, was now mixed with glee. Ginny was on the verge of victory. Ginny was going to see the cool pretender collapse. Her rival for Jack's affection was going to buckle in front of the whole school and then Jack would not want anything to do with Jane again. Looking in Ginny's eyes, Jane realised this was a momentous moment, possibly the most important ten seconds of her life.

She steeled herself inside, outwardly calmed her appearance and regained her composure. Casually, she shrugged at Ginny, turned and placed her hands palm down in the statue's upturned pleading hands. They were warm. She felt the finely carved palms under her fingertips, warm like flesh, but hard like stone. Her fingertips traced the lifeline, it was broken and short. Jane steeled herself once more, and slowly raised her eyes from his hands, up his chest to his face, and finally into his stone eyes.

"Oh!" she gasped in surprise. He was beautiful. Jane had never been this close to the statue of Alfred before, she had never dared to really look at him before, but now she did, she could see the black stone shone and reflected images of the graveyard in its shiny black surface. The carving was finely detailed and the craftsmanship exquisite, it was almost lifelike, as if Alfred had been turned to stone in a split second. She could see the pupils in his stone eyes, strong eyebrows framed them, and well-defined cheek bones underlined them. He was handsome. Then Jane realised something else, up this close she could see his expression, he wasn't pleading, he wasn't begging, his arms were not outstretched for food or scraps. He wasn't trying to save his life but rather he was accepting his death. This was his last moment, and he faced death with his arms open in welcome, and let it take him.

This realisation made her forget her fear and her current predicament—she was stood in the graveyard in front of her schoolmates, holding hands with Alfred, the shame of Middle Gratestone. Her fear returned though, in a sudden rush, a crushing avalanche of terror that engulfed her as she felt the statue's warm stone fingers move and close on her wrist. She snatched her hand back and almost fell over at the foot of the statue.

"Got you again," Jack said with a steadying hand on her wrist. She looked at Jack's hand and then up at the statue. The statue was exactly as before. Had it been Jack's hand? She questioned herself in confusion. It must have been Jack's hand, she convinced herself. Statues do not move.

"My turn now," said Jack.

"Ha, you were scared," laughed Ginny. There was no conviction in her voice now and none of the other children joined in with her mocking. They had all seen Jane hold hands with the statue and none of them had dared to do that, as far as they were aware, no one else ever had.

They whispered to each other, and looked at Jane in awe. Ginny stamped off, and Jack joined Jane, having finished paying his last respects.

"Well done Jane," he said conspiratorially. "I think we are the only two people in Middle Gratestone to have touched him."

They joined the other children outside the church gates and the teachers started to take control, calling their classes to them ready for the walk back to school. The younger classes headed off first, Jack and Jane separated and mingled with their own classmates. Soon it was Jane's turn, she smiled a goodbye to Jack, and headed off with Mr Spinner and her classmates, pausing only to look back at the statue just before it was hidden from view behind the church. It still knelt there, like a black shadow on the snow. Although perhaps the head was turned a little this way now, Jane observed, as if it was watching the children depart, as if it was watching Jane depart. She shuddered, pulled her coat around her and caught up with her classmates.

"Come on Jane," said Mr Spinner, shaking his head and banging an open hand on his ear as if trying to dislodge an errant thought. "Looking after you lot is like herding cats," he joked. Colin Moles was in the centre of the group and piped up.

"Is it lunch time yet Sir?" he asked hopefully, thinking of the jam and cream scones rammed into his sandwich box.

"It will be if we keep going Colin, otherwise you will miss it." With that everyone speeded up and concentrated on walking, the talking subsided, and was replaced with puffing and panting, as the children marched purposefully back. Before long the school gates rose out of the snow and they all rushed to lunch.

Chapter 8

Jane was cold after spending the best part of the morning outside, her nerves were on edge after her encounter with the statue. It was time for lunch so she walked into the canteen and looked around. The canteen was in one of the new wings of the school. It was brightly painted and modern. Various healthy eating posters adorned the walls, urging the children to eat sensibly and to eat sufficient fruit and vegetables. Low partitions set around the tables, afforded some privacy to those that were eating, and potted plants and shrubs, carefully positioned for maximum effect, completed the calming ambience. Children were sitting down in groups of classmates at their usual tables. Seating in the canteen followed a strict hierarchy, the youngest and hence smallest, sat nearest the kitchen from which hot meals were served on every school day except today. The older children, queuing for food, took great pleasure in mercilessly throwing insults at whichever younger child was unfortunate enough to look up and catch their eye. The oldest children, in the senior year, sat in the back corner away from the kitchen and away from the main door near which the teachers sat. There they could talk in a low murmur, unheard by the teachers and uninterrupted by the noisy energetic younger children. Only the tables nearest the kitchen were yet occupied because the children had been brought back from the church graveyard in class order. Jack and his classmates were nowhere to be seen.

Jane sat down in her usual seat with her classmates, next to the senior table, and opened her sandwich box in great anticipation. The conversation around the table was excited and revolved solely around the delicious treats harvested from the tables in the school entrance that morning. Most children had gone for a sugar rich diet that day, in defiance of the posters on the walls, and the cakes and tarts produced from sandwich boxes greatly outnumbered the sandwiches and savoury pastries. Any salad foodstuffs appeared to be totally absent. Jane recognised some of her father's pies around the table. They were each distinguished by a raised rose stuck on top and crisped brown in the oven. It was her father's trademark and appeared on all his baked goods. Her father always insisted on working late, baking for days before shame day, he spared no effort, and used all the best ingredients. 'Today it is my turn to pay the debt,' he would say. 'One day it will be yours.' Jane never quite understood what he meant but had elicited a promise from him that one day she would know everything.

Her ears pricked up as she caught the name 'Alfred' in the table conversation and so she started to listen to the boy that was talking in a guarded tone. All other conversation at the table had stopped and Jane's classmates were giving their undivided attention to the speaker. His name was David, he was strong and stocky, and his arms were muscular. His elbows were planted on the table and his shoulders were hunched up making them appear even larger. He always commanded respect when he talked, not just because of his build but because he was bright, articulate and a wonderful story teller. Jane really liked David, they did many tasks together in class and shared the same music teacher. David was a talented piano player and always encouraged and challenged Jane to practice and improve. 'If it's got keys I can play it,' he used to say. He even played the church pipe organ for Sunday service although secretly Jane suspected this was just so he didn't have to sing with the rest of them. Jane really enjoyed their time together and had she not been totally infatuated with Jack she could have fallen for David. As it was though, they were firm friends, and now she willingly put aside her thoughts and gave him her undivided attention.

Inevitably on this day the conversation had moved on from the tasty morsels and treats that were on offer, to the subject of Alfred, the shame of Middle Gratestone. There were many stories about him, some were based on absolute fact and others had been embellished each time they were told. These days it was hard to tell which was which.

"So," said David aware that Jane had looked up. "The gypsies moved onto the old 'rec' field behind the church, they set up their caravans, and big 'four by four' trucks that they used to tow them with. They had dogs and kids, and everyone was running around shouting and setting up the campsite–they were making loads of noise. The vicar had been in the church and came out to see what was going on. The gypsies were polite to him but they said they were staying there all summer and he couldn't do a thing about it." Jane smiled to herself as David spoke. Everyone knew that the vicar was David's dad but David only ever referred to him as the vicar. It was as if David wanted to try to deny his parentage even though it was common knowledge.

"Well, he called the police," David ploughed on, not noticing Jane's smile. "And they said they couldn't do anything either, they told him unless a crime was committed it was a civil matter and he should call the citizens advice bureau. Well the vicar was not a happy man and totally freaked out, the gypsies were making too much noise and he had meetings with people in the church that were just becoming impossible. For instance, he was helping Mrs Moore with grief counselling and needed peace and quiet to do so. Her husband had just left her and simply disappeared. The gypsies weren't bothered though and they said they were coming to Sunday service and they were going to sing out of tune. And they saw his posters for the Middle Gratestone name changing meeting. You know 'putting the Great into Middle Gratestone.' The vicar has had a bee in his bonnet about that for ages. He thinks the town should be called Middle G-r-e-a-t-s-t-o-n-e. Well they said they were going to come to the meeting and vote for it to be called Middle Gallstone. They said one of them had a gallstone and they could mount it on a plinth in the town square. The vicar left that night, totally distraught, he didn't know what to do." David leaned forward and spoke conspiratorially. "That night Pete Brown, he lives on Church Road, he was in bed and he said he heard shouting and screaming, things smashing, dogs barking and yelping. He said it was a terrible commotion so he got up and looked out the window. He said the gypsies were stood around the caravans, they all had branches that were on fire at one end, and they were swinging them around and shouting." David paused. "Here's the thing though they weren't just swinging them around randomly, they were stood in a circle with their backs to the caravans like they were protecting them. The dogs were tied up in the middle and were barking at something that was out there in the dark that Pete couldn't see." David paused for effect and took a sip from his water bottle. He placed it carefully back down on the table and continued his story. "Then he heard it," he paused again.

"Heard what?" questioned Jane with genuine concern.

"The terrible yapping," David over-pronounced his words. "Like a fox caught in a trap but bigger, louder and terrible. Not like a dog barking, or a wolf howling, but like a fox, louder though than he had ever heard before and deeper as if it was a huge animal." David looked around checking he still had their attention.

"What happened?" someone down the end of the table asked.

"Well," said David drawing the story out and looking slowly around the table. "Pete couldn't watch anymore, he got back into bed and pulled the quilt up over his head. He could still hear though, and he heard a man's dreadful scream, and furious yapping like someone was being savaged. 'Get him off me, get him off me,' the man screamed. Then there was a bang and it all stopped. Absolute silence, not another shout or anything, even the dogs stopped barking. Pete didn't dare look and he stayed in bed under the quilt. Well he finally fell asleep and, in the morning, when he looked out the gypsies were all gone—and they never ever came back." David lifted himself off his elbows and sat back in his chair.

Everyone else was tense now and they each looked around the table checking each other's reaction. No one wanted to appear the most scared or admit to being scared at all but there was a palpable atmosphere at the table. David was quiet now, content to let his story do the work, he looked around very pleased at the effect. Jane spoke first.

"Thanks Dave, I have to walk past the church twice a day," she said sarcastically—not thankful at all. David pondered for a moment and then replied.

"Well you must have a story to tell then, especially as you touched the statue of 'the shame' this morning." Two or three children gasped in surprise, the remainder had either seen Jane touch the statue or were in the right social circles and had found out later.

"No, but I've got a question," Jane said and left it hanging there in the air.

"Ah!" exclaimed David. "I hoped that someone would," he smiled at Jane, confident that she had spotted the unusual part of the story that he had left unexplained.

David was clever and confident. He recognised a kindred spirit in Jane and saw a keen intelligence that she so often hid behind her deep green eyes. They were a formidable team when paired in class and often produced the best work. "Go on," he invited Jane to pose her question.

"Why him?" she asked. Some of the other children looked confused. They had expected something with a little more clarity from Jane.

"Yes?" drawled out David inviting Jane to be more specific.

"The gypsy," Jane clarified. Why was he screaming 'get

him off me,' if it was an animal attacking then surely he would have said 'get it off me.'" David nodded in satisfaction and appreciation.

"Now that is the million-pound question," he replied. "Why indeed did the gypsy shout, 'get him off me?'" David leant forward again, he had reclaimed his audience, and they were now utterly transfixed. "If it was a man then it makes sense, of course the gypsy would say get him off me. But why use fire to scare a man off, people aren't scared of fire are they, animals are." David answered his own question. "So, it must have been an animal. But then why did the gypsy scream 'get him off me,' it doesn't make sense does it?" he asked. "Unless of course the animal was a man, or more accurately used to be a man, or perhaps half man and half animal, maybe someone they knew or had met. Only then does it make sense!" David banged his fists on the table to emphasise his conclusion, causing everyone to jump in surprise. "Half man and half fox and tortured by it, not in one world or the other, a horrible disfigured aberration of nature." David rolled aberration with his tongue and raised his voice and arms in a crescendo of proof. He slowly dropped his arms and looked around. Jane was the first to speak, and she did so with a half-smile and a raised eyebrow.

"Fox-man?" she questioned.

"No, no," said a boy down the table. "Were-fox," he laughed.

"Yes," cried Jane. "The Were-fox of Middle Gratestone, terror of the chicken house," all the children including David laughed.

"I'm just saying what I heard," he smiled. "Be careful on your walk home tonight," he said to Jane in his most creepy voice and winked.

"I've got a story," said a voice from down the table. It was Ben Armitage. He was a generally quiet boy but possessed a cheeky mischievous grin that hinted at the fun personality underneath. He had a small pile of food remains in front of him that he had gathered together. They were testament to his penchant for turning his favourite food–pizza–upside down before eating it. This habit invariably drew disparaging remarks from his classmates. But Ben in his turn defended his habit.

'Why place the pizza in my mouth with the flavoursome part at the top. When my tongue and all its taste buds are at the bottom. If I eat it your way, it tastes of flour and dough. If I eat it my way I get all the flavour instantly.' Ben would say promoting his method despite its obvious shortfalls.

He could never be found without his girlfriend Lottie by his side. They had been together since they had first started at the school and were now referred to as Ben and Lottie, or Lottie and Ben, and never as individuals.

"Come on then Bottie," said David, cruelly combining their names. Lottie frowned and narrowed her eyes in comic annoyance. She didn't mind the insult and admittedly had laughed like a drain when David had been caught by Mr Spinner trying to orbit the teacher at the graveyard that morning. It was a game their class played amongst themselves and David was far too big and bulky to be any good at it, but he tried nonetheless.

"Well," said Ben, concentrating on his story and letting

Lottie deal with the insult. "My dad, as you all know, is a town councillor. As part of the build up to the centenary of shame day the council formed a few committees, like councils do, to try and make shame day a success. At one of the committees someone asked what had happened to the other Alfred, because apparently there was a younger brother, and he had been in the orphanage on Church Road with the Alfred that we all know." Ben stopped for a moment and Jane jumped in.

"That's right," she said. "The headmaster told me this morning that there were three brothers, and they were all called Alfred after the father, he was called Alfred as well. One brother died in the war, one was Alfred the shame, and a third was lost to the poorhouse." Ben nodded, thankful for Jane's affirmation, and continued.

"Well nobody knew what had happened to the youngest Alfred, so my dad started trying to find out. Perhaps he had lived a happy life, and maybe had some descendants, and perhaps it would be appropriate to involve them in the centenary. Or at the very least it would justify shame day. Because how could we as a town say we were ashamed of what our town had done to one Alfred, when we didn't even know, and therefore care, what had happened to the other. So, my dad pulled the records. It had been a poorhouse originally, then it became an orphanage, and now it is the pre-school on Church Road. Some of the records were missing during the First and Second World Wars, but on the whole, they were complete. The records show that two Alfreds entered the poorhouse on the same day in 1915, one age thirteen and one age seven, so that must have been them. Their last name was given as Thatcher, and we know their father worked as a thatcher before he went off to war. There is an entry for Alfred Thatcher being expelled for theft, in January 1916, that's the Alfred that we know. But then there is not an entry for the second Alfred Thatcher leaving until 1945. The orphanage, as it was then, was full of evacuees during the war and the records are a bit of a mess. But Alfred Thatcher was recorded as leaving the orphanage and returning to London in 1945, his age was given as twelve. So that doesn't tie up, the youngest Alfred should have been 37 by then. Except that every year that they did a survey between 1915 and 1945, and there were five surveys, Alfred Thatcher was recorded as being there. Now how is that possible?" Ben opened his arms out questioningly, inviting an answer from his classmates.

"Did they record ages on the surveys?" asked David, looking thoughtful.

"No, just on the arriving and departures record," replied Ben.

"Well we have to assume it is a coincidence then," said David. "He must have left and another Alfred Thatcher arrived. After all we know of four people that were called Alfred Thatcher, why not five?" David concluded.

"Or," said Jane and then stopped herself and thought for a second. "Or," she repeated. "Perhaps some harm came to the youngest Alfred, and the poorhouse lied about it. They could have said he was still there when he actually wasn't. They would not have wanted to admit losing another Alfred, would they?" Jane looked at David, he didn't reply but nodded deep in thought.

"Tell them about the photos," Lottie prompted Ben, and everyone turned back to look at him.

"My dad did a bit more digging," Ben continued. "He found some photos of the orphanage that had been taken over the years. They were in black and white and not great quality, and no one was named on the photos, but they did show the children that were there at the time. The strange thing is they were spread over the thirty-year period and yet they seemed to show the same boy, in amongst all the other kids, in all the pictures. I've looked at them and I'm sort of ninety percent sure that it is the same boy. If the quality had been just a little better, I could have been certain. And if my dad had just given me the photo's without telling me they were spread over thirty years and told me to find the boy that was in all of them, I would have picked him out. No doubt about it," Ben concluded. David looked up and clapped his hands in appreciation.

"Now that's a story," he said loudly, pointing at Ben. "There are just too many stories about that place, and about the shame of Middle Gratestone, for there not to be something going on. A Peter Pan boy at the orphanage, why not? I believe it, definitely." Everyone around the table nodded sagely.

Jane wasn't quite as convinced as David, but she had to admit the logic did seem plausible. She pondered on the facts for a moment and then Lottie spoke up.

"Er, no," she said.

"Go on," prompted Ben.

"Er, okay," she said, but seemed even more indecisive after the prompt from Ben. "I saw something once," she offered after a pause and then stopped. David nodded in encouragement. He seemed excited at the prospect of yet another story and eager to discover what Lottie had seen. Jane watched him wring his hands a little as if he was nervous and then Lottie continued.

"I was walking past the church last week, it was evening and getting a bit dark. I was with my mum but she was talking business on her mobile, so I was just walking along looking around." Lottie moved her shoulders and arms as if walking, and looked around the room, acting out her part in her story. "Then I thought I saw something strange, an odd sort of movement, so I stopped. Mum carried on she was too busy on the phone." Lottie froze in position, continuing to act out her role. "Up in the church bell tower two sticks were waving through one of the arches at the top. You know up where the bell is." Lottie traced an arch shape in the air with an extended finger. "They were there for a second and then they were gone. They were sort of upside down tick shaped, but they were gone so quickly I couldn't be sure. I thought it was really strange that someone would be up there at all. But I carried on walking and caught up with mum, there was nothing else to see now anyway, just the tower. And then after we had passed by I realised what they looked like, what they reminded me of..." she stopped her story and waited for someone to prompt her. In unison three or four people around the table jumped in with various words of encouragement.

"You've got to tell us now Lottie, the suspense is killing me," David prompted the loudest.

"It reminded me of a spider's legs," she said. "Like legs

sticking out of a crack in the wall–like they do. And then being pulled back in when you approach. Spiders always know you are there. They're very sensitive to movement and they've got loads of eyes." Lottie stopped and Ben patted her on the hand.

"I love that story," said Ben. "Really gives me the creeps. Can you imagine how big that spider must have been to be seen from the ground? Brilliant," he complemented Lottie. She smiled at him grateful for the support.

Jane looked at her watch. "Fascinating as this all is, and before I get too freaked out, I have somewhere else to be," she said aware that lunch would soon be over.

"Later," said David. All the boys watched Jane stand, gather her things and walk down the line of tables to the door. Ben received a pointed elbow in the ribs from Lottie as he had to crane his neck somewhat awkwardly to watch Jane go. The elbow was without venom though, Lottie knew he couldn't help it and he certainly had no chance of ever going out with Jane. She felt sorry for the boys that were reduced to bumbling wrecks when Jane was present, and besides she liked Jane, they were classmates and teammates and she enjoyed her company. Let Ginny fight her she thought, that was enough trouble for any one girl.

Lottie enjoyed hockey, but she was a steady player and she felt privileged to play on the same team as Jane and Ginny. The two girls had carried the team that year and they were now set to win the league and reach the county finals. Lottie played in defence and was therefore well placed to watch Jane and Ginny at work on the field.

Ginny was the current school hockey team captain and

was fierce and determined. She physically dominated opposition players, closing them down, barging them off the ball, and frequently reducing them to tears of frustration as they found themselves unable to play. There were no lost causes for Ginny, she chased down every ball and never ever gave in no matter what the score line. Her leadership was inspiring. She shouted constant encouragement to her team mates and coordinated every move that the team made.

Jane, though slightly shorter, and less imposing, had immense skill. She was by far the better player, and could snake skilfully around the pitch, leaving the opposition flailing their sticks in the wrong direction as if they were all trying to swat a nuisance fly that buzzed unseen around them. There was no doubting that she would be the next team captain, she was the leading goal scorer in the team this year and was pivotal in its success.

Lottie marvelled at how the two girls played in harmony together on the pitch as if each knew what the other was thinking, and then treated each other with such utter contempt off the pitch. She knew it was down to their rivalry over Jack. I'm glad I've got Ben, she thought to herself and reached for his hand.

Jane reached the exit and looked at the large boards mounted on easels, positioned so that everyone could file past on their way to class. They were covered in sheets of paper and each listed an activity that the children could do that afternoon. They could watch various films, play games, read books, do arts and crafts or, on a fresh sheet only added that morning, make snowmen in the playground.

Jane had entered her name on a sheet after assembly, and now she just checked that everything was as it should be. Satisfied that it was, she turned towards the door and went to leave the canteen.

The headmaster was just in front of her, talking to one of the other teachers, Mrs March. She was a tall straight lady of ambiguous shape. Her hair was pulled back so tightly it stretched the skin at her temples. She stood cross-armed listening to the headmaster. Jane looked back at the table and caught David's eye.

"Watch," she mouthed. David nodded, aware of what Jane was about to attempt. She stood behind the headmaster, and looked back one last time to make sure David was still watching, and then slowly started to walk around the headmaster. He was a man of considerable girth, he wore a green padded tweed jacket that covered most of his stomach and provided a home for his many pens but made his large frame appear even larger. Jane passed between him and Mrs March. She was below their eye level and neither one noticed the intrusion. Jane completed the circle, and gave a 'thumbs up' signal to David as she went around the headmaster's back, and prepared for another attempt. She circled the headmaster again. This time, as she passed between the two, Mrs March looked down but didn't acknowledge Jane's presence or break the absolute attention she was giving to the headmaster. Jane completed her second circle and then lifted her hands with each index finger raised to indicate two.

"Double orbit," she mouthed to David in triumph. David shook his head in admiration and silently slow-clapped Jane's achievement as she walked with a spring in her step from the canteen. He would have to do a triple orbit to beat Jane today, and having failed at a single orbit of Mr Spinner earlier, he did not rate his chances.

Chapter 9

It was much quieter in the corridor than inside the canteen, where children having finished their lunch, chattered and laughed. As she expected, Jane was the first out and both the corridor and stairs were deserted. She had cut short her lunchbreak by ten minutes so that she could be the first into the classroom. Most days she was one of the last, and didn't move at all until the bell sounded, but today was different, and it was with some excitement that she walked away from the noise of the canteen towards her classroom. She had chosen board games for the afternoon, not because she was a great fan of them, or played them at home. But because she had seen Jack put his name down on the board game list that morning. She wanted to get into the classroom first and position herself facing the door so that Jack would see her when he came in and perhaps sit at the same table. The classroom door was open, Jane stopped quietly in the doorway and looked in to gauge which table would give her the best chance of success.

The room had been prepared, many of the tables had been pushed together to form larger areas more suited to the playing of board games. Chairs that normally all faced towards the front were spaced around each cluster of tables. Jane cast her eyes around the room and became aware that she was not alone. A dark silhouette was at the window looking out, as yet still unaware of her presence. She watched for a moment and realised it was Mr Spinner at work on something at the windowsill. Only the movement of his bony elbows and slight shrugs of his shoulders gave away his distraction.

As Jane watched, one of Mr Spinners bony hands and hairy arms came into view. The spindly fingers slowly stretched out and picked something small and black from the windowsill then retracted back in front of his body.

"Mmmm," Mr Spinner hummed in approval and smacked his lips as if eating a delightful chocolate éclair. Jane was curious and continued to watch as the spindly fingers reached out again and picked another small black object from the windowsill between thumb and forefinger. They held it for a moment allowing Mr Spinner to inspect the object prior to popping it into his mouth.

"Mmmm," he said. Jane strained her eyes but could not quite make out what the objects were. They were scattered here and there along the length of the windowsill, Jane had seen them before, and slowly, as she watched, she started to feel a little sick and her stomach heaved in protest. Instinctively she knew what he was eating, her stomach heaved again and she tensed and wretched silently. Jane's eyes widened in disgust as her mind caught up with her stomach and reached the inescapable truth that Mr Spinner was eating dead flies off the windowsill. Slowly she started to back up, not daring to breathe in case she was discovered. She turned around in the corridor and pressed her back against the wall next to the classroom door.

"Mmmm," she heard again from inside the classroom. Mr Spinner smacked his lips and Jane wretched again. Sick filled her mouth and she forcibly swallowed it back down. This is horrible, she thought, closing her eyes tight shut and pressing her sweating palms against the wall. She realised she was still not breathing and forced herself to breathe again, in small, quiet, slow breaths so Mr Spinner would not hear. What is going on today? she thought, it cannot possibly get any weirder.

She opened her eyes and found herself looking straight at Mr Cunningham. His red wiry hair was wild on top of his head and his pale blue eyes stared at her from under his bushy eyebrows.

"Can I help you Jane?" he enquired in a voice that sounded like he didn't want to help. He tried to smile reassuringly but his eyes narrowed and hardened and conveyed no reassurance at all. His smile revealed two large canines that Jane had not noticed before. They gave him a wolfish appearance and looked sharp and threatening.

"No, I'm fine thank you Mr Cunningham," said Jane forcing her voice to sound measured and even. "I was just going." She sidestepped away from the classroom door to escape. Mr Cunningham sidestepped with her and casually put his arm out to lean on the wall and bar her way. He had a rather bushy growth of stubble coming through on his chin and leaned forwards into Jane so his hairy chin was at her eye level. His skin looked red and aggravated beneath the stubble, he smelt bad, and the underarm of his shirt was damp with sweat. Jane was starting to feel very threatened and looked down the corridor for help.

"Hello Jane," a voice said and Mr Spinner appeared at the classroom door. "Have you been here long?" he asked in a matter of fact way as if he already knew the answer.

"No just got here," Jane replied pressing her back hard against the wall and trying to think how to get out of there as quickly as possible. It still wasn't quite the end of lunch and Jane didn't want to spend another second there. She was cornered by the two teachers and neither of them appeared their usual selves.

"You don't have to stand out here on your own Jane, you're very welcome to come inside and wait for the others in the classroom," Mr Spinner offered without an ounce of kindness in his voice. Jane looked from teacher to teacher, they were both attempting reassuring smiles and trying to pretend that Jane had a choice, but their body language said quite the opposite.

Then just as Jane started to feel panicked a loud cheery voice boomed down the corridor.

"Ah Mr Cunningham and Mr Spinner, just the men I want to speak to." The headmaster bowled up in unsubtle style and Jane almost cried she was so grateful to see him. Mr Cunningham dropped his arm and Jane took the opportunity to edge away.

"Headmaster how nice to see you," he lied.

"I understand you have both been in the wars today," the headmaster talked over Mr Cunningham. "The school nurse informs me she's treated more teachers than children today so I thought I had better come along and see how you both were, especially as I did not see either of you at lunch today." His last remark was barbed and both teachers looked a little uncomfortable. Mr Spinner answered the headmaster first.

"Yes, a spider bit me in the graveyard," he replied holding up a spindly arm. The web of his thumb looked red and inflamed. "Nurse Mary was kind enough to give me some cream and some antihistamines, I'm sure it will be fine," he explained. The headmaster placed a reassuring hand on Mr Spinner's shoulder.

"Do let me know if you are struggling Mr Spinner," he instructed. Jane looked at Mr Spinner as she edged away, his face was white and his stubble stood out black and vivid against his skin. He appeared gaunt and his back was hunched over, his eyes were bulging out of sunken eye sockets. He did not look well at all. "And what about you Mr Cunningham," the headmaster asked swivelling his gaze.

"Ah well I ran over a wretched fox this morning on my way to work, couldn't stop in the snow you see," he laughed a yapping high pitch laugh that Jane hadn't heard before. "I got out of the car to check if it was okay and the blasted thing bit me and ran off. Hurts like blazes." Mr Cunningham raised a bandaged hand and twisted his wrist left and right as if modelling his hand on a catwalk. "Lovely work by Nurse Mary," he complemented.

"Yes, always a pleasure to be patched up by Nurse Mary," the headmaster smiled. "I sometimes wish I was more accident prone," the three men laughed as Jane turned and walked quickly away.

She reached the canteen and was relieved to see groups of children still sat around tables laughing and joking with each other. Colin Moles was lying outstretched on his chair holding his stomach and looking a little queasy. Crumbs, jam and cream littered the table leaving a visual record of the titanic struggle that had occurred between boy and scone.

"Urgh," he moaned softly. The seats next to him were

empty, probably due to the distance the remains of the scones had covered, so Jane sat quietly down.

"Safety in numbers from now on," she said to herself.

"Uh?"

"There's safety in numbers," she said out loud looking at Colin and patting him on the knee.

"These scones weren't safe and there were lots of them," Colin replied as Jane wiped clean the hand she had used to pat his leg. The school bell cut in on their budding conversation and all the children started to tidy their things away and stand up. The noise of chairs squealing back across the floor replaced the conversations that were left unfinished. Jane joined a group of boys heading upstairs and resolved to get through the day without further incident.

Sticking to her plan she kept herself sandwiched in the middle of the gang of boys and made her way to her classroom and the board games. They arrived and noisily sat down at a table. Jane sat with them and looked down at the game on display. There was a large board and lots of thick books laid out on the table. The boys were all excitedly producing small die-cast figures from pockets, bags and even some from designer cases. There were wizard figures and witches that Jane recognised as such and all sorts of other horrible monster figures with large clubs, spears and sundry other weapons that she did not recognise at all.

"Oh God, I'm in hell," she said out loud.

"Not yet," a boy with glasses sat next to her said. "We're doing 'the gateway to hell' today. We should be in hell next week though. What character are you?" he asked. Jane raised her eyebrows and tuned him out. She took one of his figures and placed it in front of her and looked around the classroom.

Mr Spinner was at his desk marking schoolwork, Jane noticed he was marking down more crosses than ticks and hoped that it wasn't her work. He was sweating and fidgeting constantly in his seat and every now and then shrugged his shoulders and stretched his back to relieve some pain. His hands caught Jane's eye, they were clawed and the four fingers on each hand seemed stuck together. She stared as he tried to put his pen down. It resisted all his efforts to place it on the table and appeared to be stuck to his clawed hand. In frustration he wrenched it from his right hand to his left but was equally unable to release it from his left. Jane continued to stare, bewildered by what she was seeing. She had known Mr Spinner for quite a few years now and he had been her form teacher since the autumn. She had never seen him act so strange.

"We need a door opening," said the boy with glasses sat next to Jane.

"What?" Jane said, caught off guard.

"You're a thief, and we need a door opening," the boy reiterated.

"What did you call me?" Jane snapped in reply, still not quite sure what was going on and disturbed by Mr Spinner's strange behaviour. The boy sighed and explained.

"You are Snide the master thief," he pointed to the die-cast figure that Jane had taken from him, and then continued. "We need you to open a locked door so that we can get into the treasure room, can you pick the lock please?" Jane looked down at the table. Her little figure did indeed look like a thief. He was wearing a mask and was carrying a bag over one shoulder. He had been placed in front of a door. All the other little figures were in line behind him and seemed to be politely queuing.

"Oh yeah sure," she said, "no problem." She looked away at Mr Spinner again but was interrupted.

"What are you going to use?" said a boy on the other side of the table. His name was Andy, he was in Jane's year but he and Jane rarely talked, he had a wizard's hat on and seemed to be overseeing the proceedings. "To open the door," the boy explained in exasperation. Jane thought briefly.

"A credit card?" she answered hopefully, unable to come up with anything else. There was muted grumbling and discontentment around the table.

"It's the year Eight Hundred A.D. and it's the Dark Ages," Andy said amazed at Jane's lack of knowledge.

"Oh, I'll use a hair clip then," said Jane quickly and produced one from her hair. Andy looked at her and then opened his hand to reveal a multi-sided dice that he rolled across the table. Everyone looked at the dice, then up at Andy.

"No, it's still locked," he said. The boy with glasses next to Jane nudged her.

"Use your lock picking tools," he urged, speaking from the corner of his mouth.

"I've got lock picking tools?" Jane questioned, from behind her hand.

"Yes of course you have, you're a master thief," the boy confirmed. Jane looked at Andy.

"I will use my lock picking tools," she said with confidence, and a murmur of approval went around the table. Everyone looked at Andy again as he rolled the dice.

"Well done, the door is open," he said.

All the boys started talking at once and moving the figures around so Jane tuned them out again and looked at Mr Spinner. He had successfully unstuck the pen and it was now lying safely on the desk in front of him. He looked terrible, a dark shadow of stubble covered his face and his eyes had sunk so far into his head they looked completely black. He was hunched over resting his elbows on the desk, his forearms were vertical and his hands cupped facing inwards. The fingers appeared fused together and his middle fingers were elongated. "Carry on children," he mumbled, his voice cracking. He very slowly half stood, as he did so, he pushed his chair back with his legs and it fell lightly against the wall. He left it there, propped up at an angle, and shuffled out of the classroom hunched over. His upper back bulged just below the shoulder and his shirt was stretched tight over it.

Only Jane watched him go, the others were all engrossed with their games. She toyed with the idea of following him but recalled her earlier plan.

"Safety in numbers," she said out loud.

"Good idea Jane," said the boy with glasses. "We should all go in the dungeon together," he declared to the other boys. They nodded their affirmation and started to move their little figures around. The boy with glasses was looking after Jane's die-cast figure. He moved it up with all the others and sat back.

"What's your name?" Jane asked.

"George," he replied and looked the beautiful, dark haired, strange girl next to him, straight in the eye for the very first time. Her eyes were magical. They shone green and looked straight into him. He looked down quickly, totally overwhelmed and blushed furiously.

"Thank you, George," Jane said and placed her hand on his in gratitude. "You're in Mr Cunningham's class aren't you," Jane asked rhetorically. "Stay away from him today, he's in a very bad mood." George nodded and looked briefly up at Jane one last time. She turned and silhouetted her profile against the window. George tore his eyes away for fear of never being able to stop looking at her. He might be trapped forever, unable to think, unable to act or even eat. An eternity staring at the most beautiful thing he had ever seen, it would be both heaven and hell. The game in front of him came into focus, suddenly it seemed frivolous and pointless and in a moment of elucidation he exclaimed.

"I've played this too much." The other boys looked at him.

"This isn't a game," Andy said indignantly. "You don't play it."

Jane stood up and left the table and the developing discussion behind, totally unaware that she had just changed the direction of George's life. She looked around, Jack was in the back corner of the room, he had arrived before Jane and she had had her back to him the whole time. He was locked in a game of chess with another boy from his class. They were using a timer with a button on top to time their moves. It was Jack's turn. Jane pulled up a chair and sat down to watch. She positioned herself next to Jack to be in the other boy's eye line. Jack took his move and pressed the button.

"Mr Spinner is acting strange," she informed him. Jack nodded, and his blonde curly hair nodded just momentarily afterwards.

"I saw him chasing a fly down the corridor," he said without breaking his concentration or his thoughtful expression. "He had a sort of crazy look about him. He was half walking, half running, and all hunched over. He's a wild man." The other boy had lost concentration and was looking at Jane.

"Normally I like a wild man," Jane said and winked at him. The boy's jaw dropped and he hurriedly looked back at the pieces on the chessboard. Where before he had seen order now all he saw was chaos. His plan had gone from his mind and his king seemed exposed. He took hold of a pawn and moved it forward.

"I think you'll find your pieces are the white ones," Jack said moving the pawn back to its original square with a strong hand. The boy quickly moved a piece next to it and pressed the button. Jack promptly took the piece with one of his own and pressed the button. "Check," he declared.

"Mr Cunningham seems a bit off as well" Jane said.

"You're right," Jack replied. "Now is it me," he continued. "Or is his hair longer now than this morning?" The boy looked up. He wasn't sure what was more confusing, Jane's beauty, or the conversation. Either way, his mind had gone totally blank. His position on the chessboard looked hopeless so he knocked over his king in surrender.

"All done?" asked Jack. The boy nodded and stood up.

"I'm going to try something else," he said politely and left Jack and Jane in the corner. Jack beamed at Jane.

"That was brilliant," he clapped his hands quietly in applause.

"I know," agreed Jane basking in the applause for a moment before turning to business. "It's funny you should say that you saw Mr Spinner chasing flies. I cut short lunch and came to the classroom early and saw him actually eating dead flies off the windowsill." Jane paused and grimaced in memory as her stomach turned again. Jack grimaced as well but then replaced the look on his face with one that was more puzzled. Jane saw the change in his handsome features but was too involved in her story to stop and question him. "I slipped back into the corridor and then Mr Cunningham appeared and literally blocked me there so that I couldn't get away. He started questioning me, and then Mr Spinner came out as well. They both stank and I swear to God, Mr Cunningham had big dog like canines in his mouth. I thought he was going to eat me!" Jane paused again and looked at Jack, giving him time to comment. He still looked puzzled though.

"So, what you are saying is that you left lunch early?" he asked, inflecting the last word.

"Oh, come on!" Jane replied. "Is that all you think is strange?" she questioned in exasperation. "He was eating flies!" Jane repeated.

"Yes, I understand that. But you left lunch, before you had to, and went to class early." Jack spoke slowly as if working something out, and suddenly Jane realised the colossal error that she had just made. The strange behaviour she had witnessed now seemed insignificant and Jane realised she had been blinded by it. She blushed and sat back in her chair, crossing her arms as she did so, now defensive and stiff. Jane looked at Jack, furious with herself and becoming more than a little annoyed with Jack. Why did he have to be so clever? she thought. Why couldn't he be beautiful but a bit dim? that would be much preferable. A slow creeping smile spread across Jack's face and lit up the room. Normally Jane would have soaked it up in rapture but she was too angry with herself. His eyes sparkled and then took on a more mischievous slant. Jane prepared herself for the next question. She knew that he would take his time.

"You never leave lunch early," Jack stated the absolute fact that Jane knew she could not deny. "You have not left lunch early in all your time at this school. So why did you leave early today?" he asked, the smile still playing on his lips.

So, there it is, thought Jane. She looked around the classroom, and paid attention to the other occupants for the first time. She was the only girl in there, she didn't play games, and she had just admitted that she had tried to get there early. Jack continued, realising Jane was not going to offer anything in reply.

"I looked for your name this morning on the lists," he said. Jane looked at him and raised an eyebrow but didn't give anything away. "Your name wasn't there." Jack continued. "I was hoping to put my name on the same list as yours. I thought it might have been nice for us to do something together, seeing as we aren't usually in the same class. So, I didn't put my name down. I left it for a bit and then looked again later, still no name." Jack had taken on a persona. He was speaking like a detective revealing the guilty party to a nervous audience, knowing that the perpetrator of the crime was amongst them. And, he appeared to be enjoying his moment. He sucked in his bottom lip in careful thought. Then he pursed his lips, letting out a long soft breath, and then sucked through his teeth. Jane tried to remain calm but she had no doubt that she had been found out. "Finally, I couldn't wait any longer," said Jack. I had to get to class and Adam had challenged me to a chess match." Jack idly pointed at the boy that he had just beaten. "So, I put my name down. Then when I checked at lunch, whose name should be the last one on the list? Just below mine? Yours!" Jack answered his own question and pointed accusingly at Jane, identifying her as the culprit to his imaginary audience. Jane didn't reply, she just put on her bored face and let Jack have his moment. Besides, she had no defence whatsoever. "So," Jack continued. "I deduce that you deliberately waited for me to put my name down so that you could do the same activity as me. And you came to the classroom early so that you could act surprised when I came in later." Jack beamed at Jane. "You love me," he mocked softly with kindness in his voice. "You want to be my girlfriend." Jane didn't reply. Jack looked pleased, not just with his deduction but with the fact that perhaps Jane loved him or at least wanted to be his girlfriend. Jane took solace from this but decided the best course of action was to completely ignore Jack's accurate deduction and change the subject. She would not admit her feelings to Jack until he was completely clear about his own. And, she still hadn't really admitted to herself how she felt about Jack, not even when she was alone. Perhaps she should try saying the words out loud later, when she was alone at home, she thought. If it sounded right, then maybe it was true. Perhaps she did love Jack.

"So, this Mr Spinner thing, do you think anyone else has noticed anything, or is it just us?" Jane asked, sticking with her plan to change the subject. Jack smiled and pondered for a moment, as if deciding whether or not to move on.

"You know why no one else has questioned this strange behaviour," he stated rather than asked. Jane raised her eyebrows inquisitively, encouraging him to accept her attempt at changing the subject. She thought Jack might be about to start on one of his rambling theories. He often did this. Jane listened because she enjoyed the time with him and because she enjoyed pulling his theories apart afterwards. He always looked directly at her when he spoke and Jane loved to gaze into his blue eyes as his voice, deeper than most boys of his age, soothed her.

"It's because of cultural sub levels," Jack continued. "We are all on our own cultural sub level. Children, teachers, teenagers, pensioners, all of us fit in somewhere on one level. And we only see those on our level. School children only see school children, teachers only see teachers, and teenagers only see teenagers. We all look to see what our peers are doing first and only look around at everyone else after we have seen what everyone our age is doing. Mates look at mates, boys look at girls," he looked at Jane and smiled as he said girls and she smiled back, before Jack continued. "So therefore, we only see those that we want to see. You said Mr Spinner and Mr Cunningham were not at lunch so probably the only adult to see them was the headmaster and we know he was concerned about them, because he was checking up on them. But probably no one else has really seen them. And before you pick holes in my theory, because I know you are about to." Jack held his hands up and stopped Jane as she was about to speak. "I know that we have seen them and we are on a different cultural sub level to them. But perhaps we are just very mature and we are starting to move up a level, therefore we've become more aware of adults," Jack finished, satisfied he had defended the obvious hole that Jane was about to exploit. She thought for a moment.

"I might have agreed with you had you not tried to pass yourself off as mature," she replied. "Everyone knows boys don't ever really mature. Therefore, your theory must be wrong. Perhaps everyone else was just busy, that's why they haven't noticed."

Jane leant forward and placed both hands on Jacks knees. "Come on," she encouraged. "Let's go and investigate, I'll be Daphne and you can be Scooby-Doo." Jane stood and looked around the room. Everyone else was still busy playing board games.

"I don't think so," replied Jack. "I'll be Sherlock Holmes and you can be Dr Watson." He stood up, fully a head taller than Jane and followed her over to Mr Spinner's desk. The desk was a mess, books and papers all appeared to be out of order and generally spread around rather than piled neatly. Jane picked up one exercise book and another two came with it. They were stuck together with a silky white material. It was all over the desk, in some places it looked like strands and in other places the strands joined together to form a sort of web-like muslin. It was fantastically sticky, Jane and Jack had to scrape it off their hands using the edge of the desk.

"Disgusting," Jack remarked as he wiped the last remnants on his trousers. "What do you think it is?" he asked quietly so only Jane could hear. The other children were still involved in their games and no one looked up. Jane shrugged and looked towards the door. Perhaps there was a way to find out more.

"Shall we follow him?" Jane looked at Jack. He was tall, lean and strong but rather than feeling intimidated by him, his size gave Jane courage and strength, she was emboldened by him and felt like showing off a little. She always felt confident when near to Jack, and now her fear that had simmered all day was replaced with curiosity. "If your theory is correct he won't notice us anyway," she added in encouragement. Jack nodded and hid his emotions behind a flashing smile. He was a little nervous but didn't want to appear so in front of Jane.

"Yeah okay," he replied. "Ladies first though." He stepped aside in polite invitation and bowed flamboyantly.

"Oh, you are too kind," Jane simpered sarcastically and together they left the classroom without anyone noticing.

Chapter 10

The corridor was deserted. Jane and Jack stepped away from the open classroom door to be out of sight of the children inside and looked around. There were no windows, strip lights ran the length of the corridor providing light, one flickered and crackled hopelessly as it failed to match the dull intensity of the others. Notice boards and pictures created by school children lined the walls and just managed to brighten the space. The notice board next to Mr Spinner's classroom, by which Jane had been trapped earlier by her teachers, advertised the upcoming 'Putting the Great back into Middle Gratestone' meeting at the church.

Mr Cunningham's classroom door was closed but they could hear raised voices coming from the other side. They were deep male voices and logically belonged to Mr Cunningham and Mr Spinner. Jack moved forward and pressed his ear against the classroom door to try and make out what was being said.

"No, don't do that," Jane hissed quietly in alarm. "What if they open the door and catch you?" Jack pulled away and tried to look casual.

"I still can't make out what they are saying anyway." He looked around and nodded to the classroom next to Mr Cunningham's. The door was also closed but perhaps offered an alternative to standing in the corridor. "What about that one, perhaps we could go in and listen through the wall." They walked quietly down the corridor and stood outside the closed door. Jack pressed his ear against the door and Jane rolled her eyes at him.

"Stop it," she scolded quietly, smiling to take the heat out of the reprimand.

"This one sounds empty; shall I try it?" he asked. Jane looked around again and then nodded in agreement. Jack raised his hand to knock but Jane stopped him.

"No just go in, they might hear a knock next door. We'll just have to bluff it if there is someone inside." Jack quietly tried the door. It was unlocked and opened easily. As casually as he could, he put a foot into the classroom and looked around the half open door.

It was a geography classroom and was decorated with children's work and various maps. The desks were arranged as normal and the classroom looked and smelt unused. Jack checked behind the door and stepped inside. Jane quickly rechecked the corridor, to make sure no one was watching, and followed Jack into the classroom, gently closing the door behind her. She was not familiar with the classroom, having dropped geography in favour of history, and skirted slowly around the outside. Jack, slightly nervously and unnecessarily, looked under the tables to make sure they were alone. Once he was satisfied that they were, they both moved over to the wall behind the teacher's desk that adjoined the classroom to Mr Cunningham's classroom.

The faint murmur of voices could be heard through the wall, but it was still unclear what was being said. The tone sounded angry though and the men were talking rapidly, probably in argument. Jane picked a full pint glass of water off the desk.

"What about this?" she asked.

"I'm not thirsty," Jack replied.

"No," Jane whispered, stifling a laugh. "Put it against the wall and listen through it, it will amplify the sound." Jack smiled and held back his own laugh.

"Okay, get rid of the water then." Jane looked around, there was no sink in the classroom and she didn't want to risk throwing it out of the window in case she was seen. Laughter and shouting was coming from outside in the playground and it sounded like a lot of children were enjoying themselves in the snow. She pulled out one of the drawers in the teacher's desk. It was full of books, loose leaves of paper and assorted pens and pencils.

"No, not in there," Jack stifled his laugh with his hand. He was going red faced and looked like he would laugh out loud at any minute.

"I wasn't going to pour it in the drawer, I was looking for something to pour it into," Jane giggled as she looked around for a container or something else suitable. "Here you drink it," she offered the glass to Jack.

"No, you drink it," he pushed the glass back.

"I don't know how long it's been there," Jane pushed the glass at Jack again.

"Neither do I," he laughed out loud and then buried his face in his hands to silence himself as Jane pursed her lips and shushed him. His shoulders shook with silent sobs and he looked over his hands with teary eyes at Jane.

"Right that's it you're going to have to drink it because I'm not," Jane said firmly. Jack regained control and took the glass. He lifted it up to the light and inspected it. There were smudged fingerprints on the side of the glass and a skim of dust lay on top of the water.

"It's got dust scum!" he reached past Jane and put it back down on the table. "No way am I drinking that." Suddenly, as Jack straightened they were very close and looked at each other smiling, for a moment they both completely forgot the teachers in the classroom next door. It felt like they were the only two people left in the world and they held each other's gaze without discomfort.

Jane totally lost herself in Jack's eyes. She had to tilt her chin up slightly to look at him. This close, and in the light from the windows that ran the length of the room, Jack's eyes were blue and bright. They smiled at her and she felt like she could rise off the floor and float into them.

"Are they sky-blue or deep-sea blue?" Jane puzzled.

"Are what?" replied Jack, staring down into Jane's beautiful green eyes, lost in his own thoughts. Jane realised she had spoken her question out loud, and reality came back to her in an embarrassed rush.

It had gone quiet outside, perhaps the children had gone inside and were warming up–hot chocolate was available in the canteen all day today. Jane put her hand to her mouth in alarm and whispered urgently to Jack.

"It's gone quiet," she said. Jack put his ear back to the wall and listened.

"I can't hear anything," he replied sounding concerned and pressing his ear harder against the wall. Jane looked around and started to walk to the classroom door when she was stopped in mid stride by a guttural cough from the corridor just outside the door. She froze stranded in the middle of the classroom and stared at the door handle, she would surely be discovered if anyone came in. The door handle twitched and then stopped as if someone had started to turn it and then changed their mind. A muffled cough came through the door again. Whoever was just outside the door, they were stifling a cough, perhaps into a handkerchief or tissue. It must have been the coughing that had stopped them turning the handle and opening the door, Jane surmised.

"Jane," called Jack urgently but quietly so just she could hear. "Come here, quickly," he called her back to another door in the classroom.

It was the stationery cupboard, Jack had already reached it and was opening the door.

"Come on," he beckoned to Jane. He looked worried and beckoned her frantically with both hands. Jane ran over silently, treading lightly so as not to make any sound and squeezed into the cupboard next to Jack. As Jack closed the cupboard door and plunged them both into darkness Jane just glimpsed the classroom door handle turning again.

It was cramped in the cupboard; the air was stale and there was a faint smell of mould. Jack and Jane stood side by side facing the door in silence. They both tried to control their breathing and reduce their heart rates back down to normal. Their survival instincts had kicked in, as if they knew their activity risked their lives rather than just detention or a reprimand. On a normal day they would have probably accepted they had been caught and remained in the classroom to be discovered. However today had been far from normal and they both had no desire whatsoever, to face either Mr Spinner or Mr Cunningham.

Jane had her hands clenched in front of her as if praying,

she pressed her lips against her thumbs to ward against any inadvertent exclamations of fear, and waited. She could hear Jack breathing, and then from outside, the sound of the classroom door closing followed by the sound of it being locked. The cupboard door was thin and ill fitting, sound passed easily through, and Jane could clearly hear movement in the classroom. At each sound she had to prevent herself from jumping, she concentrated on remaining calm. Now that her eyes were adjusted to the darkness, she could see a sliver of light at her feet where the door did not quite meet the floor. She wished she wasn't there and wondered why she had let her curiosity get her trapped in the cupboard. Ordinarily, she thought, she might have liked being trapped in a cupboard with Jack but not today. The fun and laughter they had shared a moment ago was gone and had been replaced with a deep unsettling fear. She wanted to talk to Jack and hear his reassuring voice but here in the cupboard they might as well have been a mile apart.

The sound of a desk screeching loudly across the floor interrupted her thoughts. The noise cut through her and jangled her nerves, she felt Jacks arm move around her lower back and pull her in, and she welcomed the comfort it brought. The screeching from the desk stopped. The sound of it dragging across the floor had moved away from them, and Jane, rightly or wrongly, assumed the desk had been placed in front of the door. A second desk was then pushed across the floor. The screeching lasted slightly longer but sounded as if it stopped near where the first desk had been left. Someone was barricading the door so that no one could get in, she thought. Or, she suddenly realised, so that no one could get out.

This thought filled her with dread and her knees almost buckled. If the barricade was to trap her and Jack then they had already been discovered and all they had done was present themselves as victims. How could I have been so stupid? She rebuked herself silently.

Jane pushed the thought from her mind and counted to ten slowly under her breath. She realised she was not helping herself to remain calm by continuing to imagine the worst. And besides, they were trapped and all they could do now was wait quietly for the room to clear.

The coughing started again. They were deep wracking coughs that lasted a lot longer this time. As they finished, there was a choking sound followed by the unmistakeable sound of retching as the person threw up and vomit splashed on the floor. The person groaned and spat to clear the vomit out to breathe more easily. The voice cracked and was deeper than usual but was still recognisable. It was Mr Spinner. He groaned again and threw up once more on the floor then cried out as if in pain. His breathing was heavy and fast and he gasped for his breath in between retching and vomiting. His mumblings were unintelligible but conveyed pain and suffering as clearly as words.

Jane jumped involuntarily as a large crack sounded and cut through the air like a whip, followed closely by another and another. After each, Mr Spinner shouted out in pain, the shout was stifled as if he had his hand over his mouth. He screamed repeatedly into his gag and gasped for air in between. His lungs sounded full of fluid and his breath came in wet gasps. Another loud crack came from the room, Jane recognised the sound. It was a sound she had only heard on one previous occasion. But it was a sound that she remembered clearly.

She had been playing hockey when one of the opposition had fallen heavily just in front of her. There was a loud crack as the player's leg twisted and the bone broke. It was a terrible sound and Jane had relived the moment that the bone had broken again and again in bed afterwards. The sound was distinctive and once heard it could never be forgotten. It was this sound, the sound of bones breaking, that Jane could hear outside the cupboard door right now.

Another crack sounded out loud, it was distinct, and Mr Spinner sobbed in agony. Jane thought about rushing out to help but was frozen in terror. Her instinct told her to stay hidden from view, whatever it was that was happening in the classroom was unnatural and terrible. Jane clenched her fists and tried not to listen to the crack of bones breaking, and the sound of Mr Spinner's torture, as it carried on and on.

Time passed slowly in the cupboard and the air became thick, warm and stale. Jack and Jane remained stood stock still, as their legs grew tired, and their back's ached. Outside the cupboard door, as the hours passed, the gasps of pain became more infrequent and the heavy breathing subsided and became indistinct. The cracks continued awhile and then were replaced with lesser crunching and grinding noises. Occasionally a desk would be knocked and screech loudly across the floor in protest. Every time Jane jumped and then quietly cursed herself. She tried to picture what was happening but her imagination was unequal to the task. She dreaded what she would see if she opened the door and she had to fight a battle with herself as her curiosity almost got the better of her. Perhaps knowing was better than not knowing, she thought, as her mind tried to trick her into opening the door. However, she managed to thrust the coercing thoughts away and retain loose control.

Jack and Jane remained there for a long time, the cupboard seemed to become smaller and the air staler as they stood for what seemed like many hours. Eventually the light that peeked under the door started to dim. Jane knew it got dark at around four o'clock this time of year so at last she had an appreciation of the time. She did not know the exact time they had become trapped in the cupboard but guessed that they had been there for at least two hours. The sounds coming from outside the door had changed again. The crunching had been replaced with tapping and sounds of movement that seemed to prowl around the room. The loud breathing had stopped completely and Mr Spinner had not shouted out or grunted for some time.

Jane's feet were becoming numb. She wriggled her toes to try and get the blood flowing, and stretched her back and shrugged her shoulders. She did it slowly so as not to make any noise or lose her balance. Beside her, Jack remained unmoving, like a rock. Jane was so grateful that he was there. She couldn't imagine what this would have been like without his calming presence. And still they remained there, as the light from under the door completely disappeared and their world became pitch black. She wondered if anyone had missed them. Was anyone looking for them right now? No one had seen them leave their classroom, she was sure of that. Mr Spinner had been the teacher supervising them and he wasn't out there to tell anyone they were missing. So perhaps today, no one would notice. How much longer will we have to stand here? Jane thought. She had stopped wriggling her toes now and had abandoned them to numbness. Her back ache had been replaced with pain, and shrugging her shoulders hurt too much for her to continue.

Time continued to pass, it had been dark for at least an hour now, opening and closing her eyes made no difference to what she could see. It was hot and stuffy and Jane wondered if she would faint before her legs gave way or vice versa. A bang and the tinkle of glass falling to the floor interrupted her disjointed thoughts and brought her back to her senses. She listened intently. There was another bang and a smash. Glass crunched as if something stood on it and ground it into the floor, and then there was silence. Jane froze, and listened. Together she and Jack stood straining their ears for a very long time but heard nothing at all. Jane thought to herself, perhaps My Spinner had gone out the window? She was about to say something to Jack when he broke the silence.

"I think he's gone," he said very quietly into Jane's ear. Jane nodded automatically and then realised Jack couldn't see her response in the dark.

"Yes, I think he has," she replied. Inwardly though, she was struggling to understand why he would leave by the window. "Why would he leave by the window?" she whispered.

“Perhaps he doesn’t want anyone to see him,” Jack replied. Jane nodded, and then again remembered that Jack couldn’t see her.

“He smashed it though,” she said, knowing full well that it did not make any sense that Mr Spinner had left by the window. “How long shall we wait?” she asked Jack, hoping to put off the decision to leave the cupboard. It had felt like a trap before but she had been in the cupboard so long now that it felt safe, and perhaps it would be better to stay inside rather than risk going outside. At least they were alive and unhurt in here, and she was worried what she might find in the classroom.

“Five more minutes,” Jack whispered. “And if we don’t hear anything in that time then I’ll go out. You stay here, there’s no sense in us both getting caught.” Jane pondered on what Jack had proposed for a moment. It was brave and gallant of him but Jane didn’t think that she could bear listening to Jack getting caught while she cowered in the dark.

“No, we go out together,” she whispered back.

“You know,” said Jack. “I couldn’t help but think while we’ve been standing here about something my dad told me.” Jack paused as if waiting for Jane to ask him to continue but Jane remained quiet thinking that Jack was going to tell her something that she didn’t want to know. Jack’s father was a police officer, and whatever he told Jack was probably first-hand information, and therefore likely to be totally inappropriate given their current situation. Jack, not getting any confirmation from Jane either way decided to blunder on. “My dad said that Middle Gratestone has had lots of unsolved missing person cases over the years. People go out to the shops, or walk the dog, and just don't ever come back. There's no explanation as to what happened to them and no reason for them to leave. They just simply disappear. And it's not just happening now, it's been happening for years, and no one knows why. We're like the Bermuda triangle of England.

Jane decided not to reply and instead let silence convey her displeasure at receiving this latest information at this particular time. Perhaps all the disappeared had had cause to hide in a cupboard and it was there that they had met their fate, she thought.

They both quietened down and waited. It was quiet both inside and outside the cupboard. Jane barely breathed so as not to mask any sound from outside, and she couldn't hear Jack at all as he presumably did the same. Finally, after what she thought was about ten minutes of silence Jane whispered to Jack again.

"Let's do it," she said without conviction.

"Okay," he replied with an equal lack of conviction. Jane felt Jack move slightly and she lifted a hand to stop him.

"Wait! What shall we do if he is there? My legs are numb. I don't think I can run," she worried. Jack stopped.

"Mine too," he said. "If he is there perhaps if we just try and be quiet, it's dark, maybe we can slip past without him noticing." Jack slowly opened the door as quietly as he could. It creaked loudly in protest, usurping the silence that had reigned for so long.

They both paused and listened. It was cold in the classroom and the winter night air blowing through the broken window rushed into the cupboard bringing welcome relief. It was dark outside the school but some light from the streetlights filtered in and Jane could make out the shapes of the tables and chairs scattered around the room. They were not laid out in straight lines anymore, some had been knocked onto their sides.

Jack stepped out warily and Jane followed, casting her eyes quickly around the room. Slowly and quietly, they made their way to the classroom door.

The light was on in the corridor and it outlined the door in the dark. They reached the door without incident and set about clearing the desks barricaded in front of it. Without saying anything they each took an end and lifted the desks one by one out of the way. Jane reached out and tried the door handle.

"It's locked," she whispered to Jack. Jane swallowed her disappointment and felt around the handle for a key but the keyhole was empty. "There's no key." She checked behind her, Jack was close but everything seemed calm and quiet. "Shield your eyes I'm going to turn the light on," she said and flicked the switch before Jack could protest.

The lights flickered and then burst into life. Jane tried to look around for danger but couldn't open her eyes in the bright light. She held her hand up and tried to peek through her fingers but to no avail. She took her hand away, but kept her eyes tight shut, and allowed her eyes to adjust to the light that came through her eyelids. All the time she couldn't see, she imagined something terrible was about to attack her and rip her apart. She forced her eyes open, they adjusted to the light, and at last she could look around properly.

The classroom was a mess. Desks had been knocked over and chairs were lying broken on the floor. Over by the teacher's desk, there was vomit and blood that had been trodden in, and spread around as if someone had writhed in it. Jane put her hand to her mouth.

"Oh my God!" she gasped out loud seeing teeth and splintered bone in the congealed mess. Jack was to her left and pointed to the other end of the room.

"It's Spinner's clothes," he said. "Maybe the key is in his pocket." Jane looked over and then around the room again as if she might have missed a naked teacher.

"His clothes?" she questioned.

"Yeah, and they're all ripped up," jack replied. Jane remained where she was as Jack checked the pockets. "Got it!" he said triumphantly and flashed Jane a smile that she was very grateful to receive.

"Let's get out of here," she urged.

Jack unlocked the door and they rushed out into the empty corridor, not caring if anyone was there to see them. Jack locked the door behind them and dropped the key on the floor. Together, they ran quietly along the corridors to the cloakroom to retrieve their warm winter coats. On the way they met some of the army of school cleaners busy turning mess and tarnished surfaces into order and buffed perfection. They scowled at the two children as Jack and Jane tried unsuccessfully to walk across the freshly mopped floor without leaving footprints. Jack and Jane giggled in relief at the sudden normality and without saying another word to each other they pulled on their hats, coats and gloves to keep off the winter cold and headed for the main door.

Chapter 11

Earlier that same morning, Mr Spinner had started his day in a very ordinary fashion. By the time he left for work he was refreshed with two cups of English breakfast tea, full of energy thanks to bacon and eggs, and sporting a fresh, crisply starched white shirt under his jacket and overcoat. He was slightly surprised by the snow that had fallen overnight and had to forego reading the morning newspaper to make up for the time lost walking, rather than cycling, to work. He walked in the dark along his normal route, it was cold but the fresh snow was light and fluffy and he made good progress in his heavy walking boots. On other days, school might have been cancelled due to the snow, but today was the centenary of shame day, and Mr Spinner was certain that teachers and pupils alike would be making every effort to get to school on time. So, he pushed on, walking quickly to keep warm and left lonely footprints in the moonscape for others to follow later.

The groundskeepers were clearing snow from the playground when he arrived at school. They had started at the school end and were halfway down towards the gate. A cleared path stuck out from the school door like a black tongue, with the groundskeepers resting on shovel handles at the very tip.

"Morning Mister Spinner," the head groundskeeper greeted. "Watch yourself on the path, not salted it yet," he warned.

"Good morning, yes, thank you," Replied Mr Spinner slightly out of breath. "I will do, jolly good," he added and continued past the small gathering.

The school was mostly dark, only a smattering of lights were on downstairs and the tall pointed roof was still lost in the dark of the night. Mr Spinner hurried into the light and warmth of the hall, produced a large tin from his bulging rucksack and added it to the growing selection of tins and sealed plastic containers on display.

Mr Spinner was not a chef by any standard but he loved to enjoy a large Devon cream tea. Two scones, full of strawberry jam and clotted cream, washed down with afternoon tea was his absolute vice and he rarely missed out. Consequently, and to have a constant supply of scones, he had mastered their creation over many years and was now very proud of them.

However, he had not managed this achievement without having had a few problems on the way. The smoke alarm that his wife had insisted that he install before embarking on his long journey had been called into action many times. And the consistency of his early scones varied from rock hard stone, to something soft that remained curled in the baking tray in straight lines, as if deposited by an obsessively neat spaniel.

Experience and time had the desired effect though and once all negative outcomes had been unscientifically discounted and all possible disasters had occurred, Mr Spinner was able to create a truly delicious scone, again and again without fail. The clotted cream and jam, he bought locally from a farm shop that sold organic locally made produce. The cream was so thick it almost defied being spread, and the strawberry jam was sweet and packed full of fruit.

In total, Mr Spinner produced three biscuit tin loads from his rucksack and began to place the scones on a round cake tray, piling them up in a pyramid that resembled an Alpine peak once complete.

Mr Spinner checked his watch underneath the layers of tweed and leather and headed into his classroom to prepare for the arrival of the children. It was normally a chaotic affair, the children wanted to greet each other and share their previous night's funny stories, and Mr Spinner wanted them to sit as quickly and quietly as possible. The opponents in this battle of wills knew the game well. Mr Spinner would let the children get away with as much noise as he thought appropriate and the children would make as much noise as they thought Mr Spinner would let them get away with. It was a fine line carefully trod and the children teetered along it like tightrope walkers in a circus tent.

Today though the headmaster had given very specific instructions, to all the teachers, on how they were to greet the children on the morning of the centenary of shame day. Mr Spinner was a little uncomfortable with the direction provided and had explained to the headmaster that the pupil-teacher divide was very hard to establish and easily lost but the headmaster had insisted. So, reluctantly, Mr Spinner greeted the first pupil that arrived in his classroom that morning, Jane Rose, and everyone afterwards with exaggerated courtesy.

He was glad it had been Jane that had arrived first. She was a bright girl, and a joy to have in the class. She helped him to keep order with a withering wit that coerced unruly boys into submission. She was beautiful too and used her wit and looks in harmony, like fingers playing a guitar, to get the boys to dance to her tune. Mr Spinner marvelled at the level of control she had over the boys and knew that he could never hope for such enthusiastic obedience. Jane was a nice girl as well and overall managed to stay friends with nearly all the girls in school. He thought most girls wanted to be her, and emulate her, and that was perhaps why she was friends with so many.

Or, it could be that they didn't want to get in between her and Ginny Petherbridge, those two had been involved in a truly vicious cat fight of words and dark looks for over a year. He tried out his awkward greeting routine on Jane and not receiving any negative feedback he continued it until all his students were seated.

Mr Spinner found assembly to be an uncomfortable, turgid affair. The headmaster tried his jolly best to make it interesting, and Ginny was as engaging as ever, but Mr Spinner had taught at the school for 20 years and had heard the story of Alfred too many times to be moved by it. He also didn't enjoy standing for so long. It was necessary, he understood, the hall was too small for teachers and pupils to be seated so he suffered in silence. And descended into a reverie from which he only surfaced long enough to clap in time with everyone else before descending again and losing himself in mindless thought.

The visit to Alfred's grave was a different matter entirely. The children were excited by the snow and slipped and slid, by intentional accident, and tried to lob snowballs unseen into the air to land on other unsuspecting children. Mr

Spinner busied himself about, keeping control of the unruly mob, until what he had been waiting for finally happened. It happened so quickly in the crowd of hoods and hats milling around just below his nose that he almost missed it. One of his pupils, David, the vicar's son, attempted an orbit and Mr Spinner caught him in the act.

The pupils had been playing this game all term and the teachers had discovered it after capturing one of the children circling a group of teachers. The child had broken under questioning, and threat of detention, and confessed all. The teachers saw no harm in it though and after a discussion in the teacher's common room they had devised a sweepstake. Each teacher bet on which pupil they believed would achieve the most orbits that term. Mrs March, a tall lady who wore an abundance of clothes that completely masked her slender figure, chose Jane before Mr Spinner could do so. Mr Spinner, in his turn, chose Ben Armitage, a mischievous boy that had the subterfuge and concealment skills of an international spy and was consequently doing very well. Jane though was a master and could become almost invisible when she wanted to, she had circled many teachers, unseen by the victim while other teachers watched in silence and tallied the score.

Mr Spinner had already spotted his boy Ben circle Mr Cunningham beautifully that morning and now he had caught David red-handed. He made a great show of telling David off so the other teachers could see that he had caught him then he continued into the graveyard, behind the children, to ready himself for the headmaster's speech and prayers.

In contrast to the assembly Mr Spinner normally found this part of the day very moving. The headmaster prepared a different prayer every year and they were invariably very good. Sometimes the prayers were direct extracts from the bible and sometimes the headmaster carefully crafted them himself. The setting in the graveyard created a sombre mood that captured everyone and it was difficult not to become emotionally involved, especially when confronted with the reality of Alfred's grave, side by side with his parent's and brother's graves.

Death was such a permanent thing, he thought as he looked down at the graves, and life was so precious and fleeting. It fluttered by like a butterfly, beautiful and aimless, and then it was gone.

The headmaster began to speak and Mr Spinner listened carefully. The words struck home, they were especially poignant to him, and each line pierced holes in old emotional scars that ran deep through his soul. Mr and Mrs Spinner had lost a child of their own many years previously and as the headmaster recited the prayer, long suppressed memories rose up from the deep sea of Mr Spinner's mind. They breached the surface in random order and burst into his conscious. Mr Spinner viewed them in vivid colour and cried silently at the sudden sight of them behind tightly shuttered eyelids.

He saw his son's first birthday cake, he saw a day out on the moors in windy sunshine, he saw a messy jam doughnut enjoyed by father and son, and many other memories in quick succession. Mr Spinner couldn't bear it and opened his eyes, biting his lip hard and wiping away his tears before the prayer had finished and the children looked up. He hadn't expected that sudden rush of emotion today and as the children began to move off he supported himself on Alfred's gravestone.

A sharp pain in the web of his thumb yanked him out of his sorrowful melancholy. His mood change was dramatic. Anger swamped him and buried the memories that had recently surfaced back down into the depths. He grabbed a stick and stabbed it into a crack in the gravestone trying to smash the retreating creature as it wedged itself into the recess. Die, die, die, he thought as he stabbed again and again, blunting the stick but not his anger. The spider bite had dispelled the images of Mr Spinner's son and now it was as if he blamed the spider for his son's death. Rage stoked him up for a moment and he gritted his teeth and thirsted for the spider's blood.

"Are you okay Mr Spinner?" Jane's voice sounded from somewhere and he struggled to find it and focus on it and pull himself back from the dark place he had entered.

"Yes, Yes," he replied as he surfaced but did not look at her, for fear of revealing the darkness within himself. "Off you go, up with the others," he dismissed Jane before the tumult of emotions overcame him again. He sucked at the web of his thumb as the children filed past Alfred's statue and he looked at the black stone figure for a while. He wasn't sure if he had ever really looked at it before but now he felt compelled to do so. He stared and looked at it in minute detail, studying it like he would a painting hung on a museum wall, as if looking for hidden meaning and depth. Perhaps the artist had left a message there, and perhaps if he stared for long enough the message would become apparent. It may have been because of the snow surrounding it but the statue was incredibly black, blacker than anything he had seen before. It sucked in the light and reflected it back here and there on its curved surface. Mr Spinner sensed power in it and control. He felt like the statue was trying to tell him something. Get them, he thought.

"What?" he said out loud surprised by the sudden involuntary thought and looked around but he was alone at the grave. The last of the children were clustered around Alfred's statue, so Mr Spinner shrugged off the errant thought that had invaded his mind, stepped over the low stone wall that circled the graveyard and walked towards the children milling around in Church Road.

The headmaster nodded to him and Mr Spinner started to call his class together to get them ready for the walk back to school. He counted the children off and then strangely got stuck at number seven, as if he had forgotten what number came next. Mr Spinner counted again, this time without a problem and in doing so checked all the children were present. Most odd, he thought.

By the time he set off with his class Mr Spinner was not feeling himself. He was queasy and a little dizzy as if he had just got off a fairground ride, and until they were clear of Church Road he had a strange feeling of being watched. It was a subtle feeling, a feeling triggered by his sixth sense. He had experienced the feeling, every now and then, throughout his life however every previous time when he looked to where his sixth sense guided him, someone had been staring at him. Normally the person was staring in an idle inoffensive fashion, they were just somebody with nothing better to do than look around and take in the scenery. Today though the hairs on the back of Mr Spinner's neck stood up, as if to look around themselves, and no matter how much he scoured his surroundings he couldn't identify the person that was looking at him. Jane was the only one in the class that seemed a little skittish but she was firmly concentrating on the graveyard and not staring in his direction.

As Mr Spinner looked at her another involuntary thought came to him. Get her, he thought. Instantly he felt ashamed, these were not thoughts he was used to. He took great pride in his work as a teacher and always behaved professionally and fairly. He considered himself a decent human being and always strived to be nice and considerate to others. He didn't like these errant thoughts and didn't understand where they were coming from. He looked away from Jane and hoped that he wasn't going mad.

Colin Moles interrupted his confused thoughts with his usual question about lunch time. Mr Spinner looked at the loose gaggle of children, as their faces all turned towards him as if following a tennis ball in flight, hoping he would give them the reply that they wanted.

"It will be if we keep going Colin, otherwise you will miss it," Mr Spinner replied to get the class moving as quickly as possible so that he could get back to school and sit down until he felt better.

They continued in silence. The relaxed morning and invigorating walk to work were now distant memories for

Mr Spinner, the fresh cold air he had enjoyed earlier felt different and instead of energising him, now seemed to be sucking the strength out of his legs. He scuffed his feet along, blurring his footprints in the snow and his head and eyes dropped in surrender. Breakfast was a long time previous and a hunger started to take hold of him that needed to be satisfied. Dark thoughts filled his mind so much he thought they would spill out in a torrent of expletives if he tried to speak, and his joints ached in protest as he walked with the children.

By the time they reached school Mr Spinner was exhausted, he let the children rush excitedly off to lunch, without uttering anything to them, and he shuffled off to his classroom to sit quietly on his own. Images of Jane, Jack and Ginny kept popping into his conscious like a kaleidoscope, and all the time, underlining it all, was the number seven. Mr Spinner's rational mind knew that something was wrong.

He visited the school nurse, received some encouraging words and some antihistamines, in case he was having an allergic reaction, and then he returned to the classroom to skulk and feel sorry for himself. Why number seven, he wondered, trying to rationalise the problem and think it through. He knew seven was a naturally occurring number, repeated often across nature and theology. He read some of them off in his mind trying to make sense of it all. Seven days of creation, seven days in the week, seven continents, seven wonders of the ancient world, seven colours in the rainbow, seven celestial bodies visible from earth, seven periods in the periodic table, seven seas, and seven deadly sins. The number seven appeared in nature and theology again and again, and now it was banging away in his mind again and again, but he did not know why. Nothing he could think of explained it away and he started to wonder if the banging number would continue to repeat over and over in his mind until he collapsed into insanity.

The hunger started to eat at him again, like a rat, it gnawed and scratched at him demanding to be fed, incessant and relentless it scurried around nipping and biting until he could stand it no longer. Finally, he knew what he had to do and stood up and walked unsteadily to the window. His rational mind screamed out, begging him to stop, but the urge to eat was primeval and too strong to resist. He could see what he needed, it was just there in front of him, waiting for him to reach out and take it.

With a trembling hand Mr Spinner plucked a dead fly from the windowsill and held it up to the light to inspect. It was a common housefly, devoid of one wing and desiccated by the sun. It had lain on its back, its six legs bent at the joint and closed in on itself as if in its final moments it had adopted the foetal position for comfort before it died. He righted the insect in his grasp and looked at it eye to eye. Its body was black, run through with shiny blue lines, fine hairs stood up on its back and its remaining wing pointed upwards, veined and transparent in the light from the window. Its red compound eyes did not see Mr Spinner open his mouth and drop it in and then crunch the dry old carcass. It crumbled into bits of husk, head, thorax and leg as it broke up in his mouth. The legs found gaps between his teeth that he had to tease out with his tongue and swallow down one at a time. It tasted delicious and Mr Spinner hummed in approval, totally lost in delight and oblivious to his surroundings.

"Mmmm," he approved and picked up another. Somehow it seemed preferable to him that the legs got stuck between his teeth, it meant the fly lasted that little bit longer, as he wormed the legs out and swallowed them down. Why had he not tried fly before? He thought. They were delicious and easily found. He popped another tasty treat in his mouth. This one was fresher and as he bit down the fly popped and the juice burst out. He rolled his tongue around savouring the flavour and mixing the juice with his saliva into a succulent paste, which he then sucked down, and smacked his lips in total rapture.

There were more dead flies trapped between the double-glazed windows, Mr Spinner retrieved them and spread them out on the windowsill and then worked his way down the line of bodies. One at a time he picked them up, inspected them, popped them into his mouth, and then hummed in approval. Some were crunchy and some were juicy. Like eating chocolates, from a selection box without the contents list, he didn't quite know what to expect next. He continued in enjoyment only stopping briefly, every now and then, to dislodge a stubborn leg from between his teeth with a fingernail when his tongue was unequal to the task.

A voice from outside the classroom door interrupted him, it was Mr Cunningham. The voice brought Mr Spinner back to reality, and then the next voice that spoke sent him back into his crazed world, of voices in his head and insatiable hunger.

It was Jane. He had to get Jane.

He shuffled quietly to the door and joined an uncomfortable looking Jane and a dishevelled Mr Cunningham in the corridor. He tried to convince Jane to join him in the classroom but a pain between his shoulders blurred his thoughts and caused him to grimace in what he thought probably looked like a snarl. He was about to give up on persuasion, and take a more direct approach, when the headmaster arrived and started asking irritating questions. As he answered the headmaster's questions he watched Jane sidle away in his much-improved peripheral vision. Patience, he told himself. Let the little fly buzz around, sooner or later she will come to the hungry spider. Mr Spinner listened to the headmaster and bided his time.

The afternoon was hazy. Mr Spinner's thoughts jumped in between the rational, what should he do, to the irrational, how to satisfy his hunger. He tried to mark exercise books but his thoughts kept wandering on their own accord. Get Jane, he thought. No, he thought back, and wrote down a cross in a book. Get Jane, he thought. No, he fought back and entered another cross. Get Jane. No! He entered another cross. All the time that he was looking at the exercise book, he was also able to look at Jane. His eyesight had changed and he found that somehow, he was able to focus on the exercise book at the same time as he was focused on Jane. Multiple images filled his vision and he absorbed the vista on display around him. He studied Jane looking back at him and he looked at the books as if he had more than one pair of eyes. Finally, just as the urge to eat became overpowering, and the need to grab Jane took him completely, he stood and headed for another classroom to see if he could find some more flies. Perhaps they would satisfy his craving for flesh.

Mr Cunningham did not seem best pleased to see Mr Spinner when Mr Spinner entered his classroom. He snarled at him, baring his sharp pointy teeth and raised his voice incoherently. Mr Spinner was unsure if Mr Cunningham was telling him something or barking at him. The two tried to communicate but the more they tried the angrier and more frustrated they both became. Mr Spinner tried to get to the windowsill but Mr Cunningham appeared rather territorial and wouldn't let him near it. The pain in Mr Spinner's shoulder blades was becoming unbearable he was hunched over and felt very sick. I need to be alone, he thought and left Mr Cunningham defending the windowsill and exited the classroom to go to the classroom next door.

A coughing fit seized him as he reached the door of the second classroom and he stifled it with his hand. His palm was covered in sticky material that was exuding from his skin. It acted like a cloth and muffled his cough and left a tacky residue on his face. He staggered inside, locked the door and pocketed the key, then for good measure he pushed two desks up against the door to barricade himself in. His last coherent thought was that whatever was happening to him he had better be alone when it happened. So, like a wounded animal looking for somewhere to die, he curled up under a desk and waited.

For the next few hours all that Mr Spinner knew was pain. He felt as if he was being turned inside out. His body was wracked by torment and he writhed in blood and vomit as cramps and spasms took him. He felt his skin split and burst and his bones break as he changed. His mind shut down to spare him the knowledge of what was happening but the pain found him in the corners of his intellect and stabbed at him mercilessly. His skull cracked open and his jaw shattered and splintered. His rib cage opened, spilling out his insides, and he morphed into something different. Something that wasn't human. He changed into something that had a purpose and the patience and the means to fulfil that purpose. He changed, and when the pain stopped and the change was complete, the creature that used to be Mr Spinner devoured the remains of skin and flesh that were left scattered on the floor. Finally, its hunger temporarily sated, the creature that used to be Mr Spinner prowled the room looking for a way out to fulfil its dark purpose. Not finding a clear route, it pressed its mass up against the classroom window. The glass cracked like a spider's web and then broke under the pressure, shattering and tinkling to the floor. The creature left through the window, climbed down the outside wall, and disappeared into the night to hunt.

Chapter 12

In the end, Jane and Jack were the last pupils to leave school, only the cleaners and one or two late working teachers remained. The two friends stood together in the doorway and looked out across the playground, it was dark now but the school lights still blazed and lit up the way to the school gates. The cleared pathway had dried out in the sun, and the black tarmac was now clearly visible. Elsewhere the snow remained but was mostly trodden down. A crowd of snowmen of different shapes and sizes were spread out in loose formation guarding the way to the gate. One carried an umbrella thrust under its arm, and another was topped in a red bobble hat. Another in a blue scarf had a snow-dog, complete with lead, stood next to him waiting for a walk that would never happen.

The silent unmoving crowd stood in the cold as testament to the children's fun and industry that day. The joyous atmosphere in which they had been created had gone with the sun. Now in the light from the school they cast long shadows that Jane's imagination filled with hidden traps and lurking danger.

The day had been strange and unsettling, Jane felt uneasy and couldn't restrain her mind, it jumped from one imagined danger to the next and fuelled her fear. She reached for Jack's hand. They both had their gloves on and were well wrapped up against the cold. Jack welcomed the contact and held Jane's offered hand, he felt braver because of it and ready to take the initiative. With a quick squeeze he gently tugged at her and led her down the steps leaving the sound of clanking mop buckets and sliding tables behind. They walked dead centre down the cleared path in the snow and looked behind each snowman they passed, into the shadow it cast on the uneven, well-trodden, snow. Slowly and carefully they got to the school gate.

Jane looked back at the school, the lights were bright and the snowmen were silhouetted against them. Their features were dark and secretive in the shadow, and they reminded Jane of the statues in the graveyard that she had to pass to get home.

"Will you walk me home please Jack?" Jane asked hopefully. "I can get my mum to give you a lift back to yours, she won't mind," she added also worried about Jack's safety.

"Okay no problem," replied Jack looking up and down the quiet roads outside of school.

All the parents and other children had left. The hustle and bustle of the school pick up had ended; all that remained were footprints in the snow, and one car. The car was just up the road with its lights on, and was parked half on the road and half on the path. Jack led Jane over the road and along the path towards the stationary car. Now directly in front, the lights dazzled them both and they looked down defensively, focusing on their feet and the path just in front of them. The snow had started to ice in the cold night air, and crunched underfoot. That and the sound of the car engine humming up ahead were the only noises.

Their breath came out in easy clouds that passed behind them as they walked forward hunched over and eyes down.

They passed in front of the car and as the dazzling lights disappeared they both looked up and stopped. It was the car door that had forced them to stop. It was fully open and blocked the path. Jack released Jane's hand and moved around the open door and looked inside, the interior light was on and the keys were clearly visible in the ignition. The heater fan was blowing hot air and Jack could feel it hot on his face as he leant in. Not seeing anyone in the front seats he looked through the back window but the car was empty.

"It's Ginny's mum's car," noted Jane, walking slowly around, eyeing it as if it would drive off on its own.

"Ginny's schoolbags are on the back seat," Jack reported.

Jane completed her circle of the car and found herself back at the open car door. She placed one hand on top of the door, as she skirted around it for a second time, and her glove stuck fast. Momentarily, her arm was pulled back and then her hand came free and left the glove behind attached to the top of the car door. Jane reached up and pulled the glove off the door, long sticky tendrils stretched out as she did so, unwilling to let the glove be reunited with its owner.

"Yuck," she said as the glove came free. "That is disgusting." She wiped the glove on the car roof trying to scrape the substance off as Jack watched, then put the glove back on to prevent her hand from freezing.

"That's the same stuff we saw on Spinner's desk," Jack said. Jane nodded and looked around nervously.

The road behind the car was darker, Jane moved slowly towards the darkness, and looked carefully, allowing her eyes to adjust. She could just see the crossroads in the distance. Houses sporadically lined the road up to the crossroads and light from them held the darkness back here and there. All seemed clear and quiet.

"I can't see anything unusual," said Jane. "Maybe we should get to my house, and my mum can phone Ginny's mum." Jack didn't reply so Jane turned back to the car, perhaps he had leant inside again. Jack's bag was on the floor next to the open door but he was not inside and Jane could not see him. "Jack?" she said a little louder. There was no reply. "Jack," she said again almost shouting, and starting to feel distinctly nervous.

Jane looked around rooted to the spot but there was no sign of Jack. Reaching inside the car she turned the ignition key and the engine fell silent.

"Jack?" she said again and then listened for a reply or the tell-tale crunching of feet in the icy snow, but her shout was only answered with silence. Jane strained to hear something more, she held her breath and listened intently, she could just hear some traffic in the far distance and a dog barking a long way off but there was no sound of Jack at all.

The beating of Jane's heart became loud in her ears and she realised she was still holding her breath. She exhaled slowly and then gratefully gulped in the fresh cold air. It hurt her throat and burnt her lungs but the beating in her ears receded. She was just about to move when she heard a faint thud behind her.

Jane sprang around, ready to berate Jack, but he wasn't there and she could see nothing to explain away the noise. She remained motionless, her eyes wide open trying to make the most of the scarce light and listened intently again.

Uncertainly, she cocked her head as if trying to locate something she couldn't quite hear and then heard the same thud sound again. Jane looked, alerted by movement in the corner of her eye, just in time to see a lump of snow fall onto the ground from a branch in the tree above her.

It was an old oak tree, its trunk was huge, and its branches thick and far reaching. On the one side they spread high out into the road, pruned at the lower level by passing traffic. On the other, they reached out over the wall next to the path and into the garden beyond. The gnarled trunk was knotted and ravaged by time and the attentions of love struck teenagers. Countless initials had been carved into the wood over the years and left there, lasting far longer than the love that had been professed.

Another lump of snow dropped to the ground, this time Jane saw it clearly and looked up into the tree to its origin. It was dark within the twisted branches and Jane struggled firstly to make out anything at all and secondly, to make sense of what she thought she could see.

A bank of six shiny, black, unblinking eyes stared down at her, underneath the eyes, two long black fangs dripped with thick mucus, and beneath them, held in two or three long black spindly legs, she could see Jack, slowly being turned and cocooned in a shiny wet web. Jane gasped in disbelief and horror, she was unable to understand what she was seeing and yet at the same time she understood completely.

Jack had been caught by a giant spider and was being covered in web to keep him trapped until the spider was hungry. She could see the green of Jack's thick duffel coat through the web, his hood was up and she was unable to see his face, but he wasn't struggling and Jane guessed he had been poisoned by those long fangs.

"Jack!" she shouted in anguish and took a step forward not knowing what to do but needing to do something. The spider had stopped turning Jack now and just held him with its long spindly legs, the eyes appeared to look everywhere at the same time and Jane knew it was watching her. She stared back frightened, angry and frustrated.

She knew now that she loved Jack, perhaps she always had, but what could she do against a giant spider? The frustration was overwhelming and in a sudden rush, her anger surged up, she grabbed a lump of hard icy snow from the path and threw it up into the tree. It hit a branch and shattered into tiny icy crystals that showered the unmoving spider. Undeterred and buoyed up by her anger she threw again and again.

"No," she shouted as she threw. "You can't have him. Let him go." Jane threw and threw and then inevitably hit the spider square in the bank of black shiny eyes. It recoiled and Jane knew then that she could hurt it. "Did you like that?" she shouted and threw again. The spider started to back off and move along the branches to the garden wall, taking Jack, cocooned and helpless, with it. As it moved something dropped from the branches into the snow below.

"Oh no you don't!" shouted Jane seeing the spider was making for the wall, and moved to cut it off. She continued to throw icy clods and started to register more hits. The spider was undeterred though and moved steadily through the branches and over the wall. Jane watched the last leg disappear and stood there breathless and alone on the path.

There was no happiness left in Jane's world. When she and Jack had left the games classroom hours earlier, and gone in search of Mr Spinner, she had been excited. She had thought that together they could solve a mystery. Perhaps they would discover a secret that would be theirs to keep and for no one else to know. But the reality had been very different, they had only found fear and monsters. Jane had borne the weight of the experience with Jack's support, but now he was gone she felt crushed, bereft and totally alone.

Looking around Jane wondered what to do, and then in sudden recollection she rushed forward and looked for the object that had fallen from the spider. She dropped to her hands and knees and brushed away the snow.

Just as her hands started to get cold through her gloves, she found a silver strapped watch encrusted with ice. She cleaned it off and held it up trying to find sufficient light to look closer. Unable to do so in the gloom, Jane jumped up and ran over to the car, to use the interior light to inspect her find more closely.

She recognised the watch and turning it over her suspicions were confirmed. There was an inscription on the back that read 'To Brian with all my love.' Jane's teacher's first name was Brian and she hissed his name.

"Spinner!" Now the watch, and the sticky web, found on Spinner's desk and the car door, linked Spinner to the spider. His behaviour had been very odd in school and Jane now realised that the spider had not appeared from nowhere, it was Mr Spinner transformed into a spider. She rechecked her logic but unbelievable as the answer seemed she could not fault it.

Jane thought on, Mr Spinner had been bitten by something at Alfred's grave that morning and had started to appear ill after that. It must all be connected she thought, and therefore to find Jack that was where she must go. It was the one place she did not want to go, the place that she had enlisted Jack's help to walk past because of her fear. The one place she never even dared to look at when she was on her own. And yet she would now have to go to the graveyard and try to find Jack there. She didn't know what she would do when she got there but she had to try, and at least she knew that the spider could be hurt.

Jane swallowed her fear and began to set her mind and her will in stone, like she always did whenever she played hockey as part of her pre-match routine.

"I will win," she said out loud. "I will win," she said again, her voice becoming more determined and calm. "I will win," she said again, forcefully, absolutely convinced that she would.

Calm now and thinking clearly, she opened the back door of the car and took Ginny's hockey stick from the back seat. She then clicked the car boot button on the car keys that were still in the ignition and looked inside the boot for anything else that might be of use. Amongst the shopping bags, raincoats and umbrellas, she found a head torch that she strapped on over her hat, and she found a socket and wrench set. She discarded the wrench but stuffed her large coat pockets with the metal sockets. They would make far more effective missiles than the icy snow.

Then, knowing she did not have a moment to lose, Jane ran to the crossroads and turned into Church Road.

She paused there and surveyed the scene, on the right she could see the church with the graveyard beyond, and on the left, was the row of colourful cottages. It was dark but light spilled from the cottages, lighting up the lower part of the road. The church looked large and forbidding, and dominated the scene. The tower was unlit and thrust up into the dark sky. Backlit stained-glass windows on the main building shone with colour and projected their depictions onto the snow-covered ground in arched patches. Stone carved figures of wise men and prophets adorned the side of the building, and in the gloom Jane could not tell if they were sculptures or real. The stonework was weathered and dark but highlighted and edged in places with white snow. Instead of admiring its impressive beauty Jane studied it for any sign of threat or danger.

Content for now, she turned the torch on, gripped the hockey stick and started to walk slowly down the centre of the road, keeping away from the trees that lined it. Tree branches reached out over the path alongside the road and Jane looked up into them for any sign of Jack or the spider. The head torch created shadows of the branches that moved and stretched on the wall behind as Jane moved along. The twigs at the end of each branch appeared on the wall as bony fingers that reached out as the light from the head torch passed by as if to catch an unwary victim.

A slight sound to her left alerted Jane, so she stopped in her tracks, and looked sharply towards where the sound had come from. The head torch followed the direction of her eyes as she turned and lit up an area at the bottom of the wall just back from the path. Two eyes reflected the torchlight back at her. They were set wide apart, and narrowed to slits as they adjusted to the bright light. Jane gasped in horror as the torch light revealed the creature. It was covered in reddish brown hair, except for on the chest, where a thick mane blazed white. It was fox-like, but much larger and heavily muscled, the shoulders were hunched and tensed as if the creature was about to spring.

It was the creature's head that had drawn the gasp from Jane. The snout was shortened and the face much flatter than that of a fox, morc human like, and for a moment Jane thought she recognised the creature, the wiry red hair set on top of the head like a mop gave it an untidy look that seemed familiar. But she shrugged the thought off as the creature's lips curled in a snarl to reveal sharp teeth.

It shifted its weight and growled a deep aggressive growl that rattled around in its massive chest. Jane knew it was about to attack and quickly reached inside her coat pocket and pulled out a large socket. She threw it as hard as she could at the creature's head. It danced to one side but still received a glancing blow on the shoulder and grunted in surprise.

Jane was already gone, running at full speed, up the hill. She turned right at the crossroads in the direction of the school without looking back. The hockey stick was gripped tightly in her left hand and she pumped her arms to run faster, her breath was coming quick now, but she felt a surge of power, as adrenalin gave her strength. The snow beneath her feet crunched loudly as she ran and obliterated any other sound. She had no idea if the creature was far behind or about to sink its fangs into her shoulder.

As she reached the car she dropped the hockey stick and dived in through the open driver's door, climbed over the handbrake, on to the passenger seat, and grabbed hold of the passenger's door handle ready to open it. Only then did she look back.

It was cold in the car, now the engine was off, and as Jane breathed hard, clouds of her own breath obscured her view. The interior light, and her head torch, created reflections on the inside of the glass that made looking out even more difficult. And despite craning her neck around, she could not see the creature. Soon, she stopped trying to locate it and focused instead on the open driver's door. She stared unblinking at the opening, waiting for the creature to attack.

Time passed slowly, she had no idea how long she sat there in the car waiting, but her breathing slowed and the windows started to steam. She listened intently and as her breathing calmed, the silence around her was revealed. Jane didn't move a muscle. She kept her hand on the passenger door handle, and her eyes on the open driver's door. She was certain this was her only chance because she was no match for the creature in the open. But as time passed and there was no sign of it Jane began to doubt it was still there.

What about Jack, she thought, he was out there somewhere all trussed up. Perhaps he was being eaten right now! Jane bit her lip.

"Concentrate," she scolded herself and stared at the door. "Concentrate," she said again quietly and slowly.

However, despite her efforts to convince herself to concentrate, she blinked and looked away momentarily. She didn't know why, perhaps she caught a movement in the corner of her eye or heard the slightest of sounds. But she looked away, and in that moment, it came for her.

It came from behind, and slammed into the open driver's door, its claws scrabbled on the snow as it attempted to gain purchase on the slippery ground and use its power to attack. Its teeth were bared, they were sharp and dangerous, and one bite would be enough to inflict a devastating wound. In a rush its back legs gained purchase and thrust it into the car.

The moment the creature struck the open door, Jane pulled on the handle on her side, and banged the passenger's door open with her shoulder. She rolled out into the snow as the creature came over the seats, and slammed the door in its face as it tried to follow her out. Screaming in terror she ran around the front of the car and banged the open driver's door shut, trapping the creature inside. She screamed at it through the glass, a prehistoric, angry, aggressive scream. Born of fear and triumph, she screamed again and again. The creature stared back with pale blue eyes, it didn't attack through the glass, and Jane realised it knew the glass was there.

She had a sudden thought that maybe it could open doors, and so grabbing the hockey stick, fled back to the crossroads. Once there, Jane stopped and first looked back and then down the road. The fox creature was still in the car, she could see it moving back and forth as if looking for a way out.

It had attacked in silence. There had been no loud, barked warning like a dog, just purposeful, measured ferocity. Jane had no doubt that the creature had meant to kill her, and she shuddered at the thought of what might have happened.

Church Road was quiet. Jane moved to the centre as before, and started to walk down the road, carefully looking up into the trees for any sign of Jack or the spider. There were lights on in the cottages and Jane thought about knocking on doors for help but didn't know what she would say.

"A giant spider has captured my friend and taken him away, can you call the police for me please." She tried it out loud to see what it sounded like and instantly dismissed the idea of knocking on doors. No, until she found Jack she was on her own. Besides, time was precious and she had wasted enough already. She gripped the hockey stick tightly and walked down to the church gate.

Chapter 13

Light spilled out from the church, dimly lighting the graveyard beyond, Jane could see some of the whiter statues amongst the gravestones, but the black statue of Alfred was lost to her in the gloom. The faint sound of organ music came from deep within the church, it lent an ominous, operatic feel to the scene and Jane was reminded of the black and white horror films she often watched with her father. She was aware of how the music in those films was used to great effect, and now here in the graveyard, every time the music built up to a crescendo, she expected something to pounce on her from behind a gravestone.

Gritting her teeth, Jane walked forward through the maze of graves to where she thought she would find the statue of Alfred. The head torch lit the way and she moved her head back and forth to light up all the shadows from where sharp toothed danger could spring. All the graves looked similar in the gloom and the small circle of light from the head torch did nothing to help Jane gain an appreciation of her whereabouts. She rounded a tall angel, with wide outstretched wings, expecting to find Alfred knelt on his plinth but there was nothing except trodden snow and dark patchy earth. Slightly confused she got her bearings from the church and walked deeper into the graveyard.

Another tall angel with wide outstretched wings barred her way. Jane stood on the plinth, on which it was mounted, and raised herself up to gain height and perhaps get a better view of where she was. The angel was icy and slippery and

Jane's hold was precarious. She felt vulnerable there on her icy vantage point, and understood her head torch was now flashing around the graveyard at height. It would be visible to anyone or anything that wanted to do her harm. But she had to do this, she told herself. Time for Jack was running out so, willing to take the risk, she continued to look around. A flash of shiny black caught her eye and she realised that the statue of Alfred was just behind the angel she was balanced on.

Jane climbed down and rounded the statue of the angel and there in the torchlight knelt Alfred on his stone plinth. His shiny surface was as black as oil. His stone eyes stared blankly at Jane and reflected the beam back at her. Jane shuddered, as she always did when near the statue, and now an irrational fear of the unknown, replaced the very real fear, she had felt during her encounter with the spider and the fox creature.

Jane looked around for some inspiration or clue as to what to do next. She had been very sure that getting to the statue was the right thing to do. She was sure that Alfred was the key to the events that had unfolded but now she was here, she had absolutely no idea what it was that she should do. Perhaps she had thought it would be obvious. Perhaps she had thought that there would be a giant spider's web here and she could release Jack or something else equally easy to work out. But now she was here, there was no clue at all and she was at a loss. She searched around looking behind statues and gravestones and then intuitively decided to do what she always did when she was stuck, when she encountered something that she couldn't solve on her own.

She would ask someone.

Jane hesitantly raised her hands up to Alfred's statue's hands. She held them there for a moment, deciding if this really was sensible, and then took her gloves off and placed her hands palm down in the statue's upturned hands. They were warm like last time but this time Jane was grateful for it in the cold of the night. She looked up into the statue's eyes. Alfred's face was unmoving, the black stone unsympathetic and hard. The expression was the same as before, the first time Jane had placed her hands in Alfred's. But then it would be, she thought. He's made of stone.

Jane searched the statuc's facc looking for something different - looking for a clue. The organ music coming from the church was building in tempo and Jane felt her fear rising with the music as she stood there. Absolutely nothing happened. The statue of Alfred, being a statue, remained unmoving. The night remained cold and quiet, apart from the organ music, and Jane remained alone in a graveyard holding hands with the statue of a long dead boy. What did she think would happen?

"Come on," she said under her breath. "Come on," again, urging something to happen. The fear was starting to take hold of her. She recognised it and tried to push it away. It was the fear of the unknown, the fear of not knowing what was about to happen but certain that something terrible was about to. The fear she felt when she watched those black and white horror films, tightly gripping her father's hand, as the next innocent victim fell into the evil monster's trap. The organ music was powerful now and Jane was breathing heavily even though she had not run for some time.

Then the head torch started to flicker and the face of the statue swam in front of Jane's eyes. She lost focus on Alfred's eyes as the light went on and off. Resisting the temptation to bang the head torch Jane kept her hands in Alfred's, and tried to see him in the flickering light.

Then, in a sudden rush, she felt it. It was an emotion she had never really felt herself, and had rarely seen it in others. But she recognised it instinctively and recoiled as if slapped.

It was rage. It poured out of the statue, she felt it through the hands that burned hot now and saw it in the eyes that glowed red. Jane looked away for fear of being blinded the eyes were so bright.

"Baker's daughter," a voice laden with scorn and hatred recognised her. It was a young voice, a boy's voice, but edged with suffering and restrained rage. Jane looked up at Alfred's face again, the statue was still there, black and unmoving, but a ghostly, ethereal face, in red light covered the stone like a mask, and lit up the surrounding graves. The eyes glowed bright, and the mouth sneered in contempt. The face leaned out of the statue and stretched at the side as if held by the black stone. It was a strain, and Jane realised Alfred was trapped in the statue, unable to wrench free.

"You will burn baker's daughter," the mouth moved but the voice seemed to come from all around her. "You will burn and suffer in hell, and I will live in your place and dance on your grave." The voice sounded certain, as if Alfred were stating a fact, and not making a threat. "Burn baker's daughter, burn," the voice repeated.

Jane let go of the stone hands and took a step back. The

ghostly red figure leaned forward and tried to wrestle free, the hands stretched out as if to grab at Jane and wrest her back but could not break free from the statue. Jane wasn't sure what she had expected from the statue of Alfred but she was certain that this wasn't it. Certainly, in life he had been wronged, but not by her, and the rage that was being directed at her, she felt sure was unwarranted.

"Where's Jack?" Jane demanded, preferring to ask what she had come for rather than dwell on what Alfred had said to her, and on how he knew her. Was Alfred predicting she would burn, did he know she would burn, or did he want her to burn? Jane didn't want to think about it but all the questions continued to rush distractingly around her mind. How did he know her? She wondered.

"Where is he?" Jane demanded, determined to find Jack before the giant spider sucked the life out of his helpless body.

Jane backed up a couple of steps to make sure she was out of Alfred's reach and looked around her, very aware that she had been totally focused on Alfred and had not paid any attention at all to anything that might have been quietly approaching from behind her. The snow on the gravestones was tinged red in the fiery light emanating from the statue of Alfred, it was starting to melt in the heat coming from him and dripped like blood onto the graves below.

"Where is he?" she said again, firmly and looked straight into his bright, rage filled eyes. Alfred smiled malevolently.

"My friends have him," he replied.

"What friends," Jane pressed.

"These friends," Alfred opened his arms wider and looked to his left.

A black jointed leg came over the top of a gravestone to Alfred's left. It was followed by another and then another. They were hairy and had sharp barbs on the end that scratched at the gravestone as they pulled the creature into view. A bank of black eyes and sharp fangs rose slowly and menacingly. The spider hoisted itself up and stood across three gravestones towering over Jane. Its two hairy mandibles glistened and dripped with mucus, as they twitched in anticipation.

Jane reached into her coat pocket and pulled out a socket, from the tool set she had retrieved from the car boot earlier. She lobbed it underarm just up in front of her and then swung the hockey stick as hard as she could. The stick connected with a loud crack and fired the socket towards the spider. It sailed over the spider and on into the night. The spider scuttled around to see where it had gone and then scuttled back.

Jane was no longer there but could be heard crunching through the snow as she ran, weaving around and dodging gravestones as she went. The spider set off in pursuit, its eight legs carried it across the top of the gravestones at remarkable speed, as it followed the noise of its prey's weaving path through the graveyard.

Jane kept the church on her left as she ran, using the lit-up stained-glass windows that she caught glimpses of through the maze of gravestones, to keep her direction straight. She held the hockey stick across her body to keep her balance on the slippery ground, and used the light of her revived head torch that had burst back into life as she moved away from Alfred, to dodge the gravestones.

Darting this way and that she nimbly made her way to the road. She looked up as she drew to the edge of the graveyard and instinctively looked left and right for traffic. The circle of light from the head torch moved up as well and consequently she completely failed to spot the low graveyard wall.

Jane hit it at knee level and her legs were taken out from under her. She crashed into the icy snow on the path and landed heavily on the hockey stick held across her front. The stick drove into her stomach and knocked the air out of lungs in a whoosh, like a balloon deflating. Deprived of oxygen and stunned by the crashing fall Jane tried to stagger to her feet but only succeeded in falling again. She heard a sound behind her and felt something take a firm grip on her shoulder. She had no air in her lungs, and her mouth opened in a silent scream that was unable to split the night. She struggled weakly, fully expecting the spider's fangs to puncture her back at any moment and fill her veins with paralysing poison.

"No," she mouthed silently in anguish and terror, and in one final act of defiance pulled the hockey stick from under her and flailed it wildly, hoping to hit the spider.

"Easy," said a man's voice from behind her. "You've had a fall." The firm grip on her shoulder pulled Jane around and she found herself looking up at a man that she recognised. "Oh, turn that off," said the man shielding his eyes from the bright light of the head torch.

He was the large man with the wind problem that lived in the cottage at number seven Church Road. Jane had never been so glad to see him as she was now. Her breath came back with a gasp and as she breathed air into her starved lungs her strength returned. Quickly she looked around for the spider but she could not see it, and with a little help from the man got to her feet.

"Thank you," said Jane looking up at him. He looked away and pointed to his forehead.

"Head torch please," he repeated.

"Oh sorry," replied Jane but rather than turn it off she pulled it from her head and flashed it around to check that the spider was gone.

"You took quite a fall. Are you running away from someone?" the man asked looking towards the circle of light flicking from shadow to shadow. Jane realised it was rather obvious that she was looking for someone or something and so turned the torch off and stuffed it in her pocket.

"No just running to keep warm," she lied, not sure why. She brushed the snow off and patted herself down checking she was not injured. Her shins hurt but everything seemed to be working as expected. "Do you have a mobile phone? Perhaps if you don't mind I could phone my mother and ask her to come and pick me up." Jane kept her voice level. The man looked at Jane for a moment, pondering on the question she had asked.

"No, I'm afraid not. But my home is just here and I have a house phone, perhaps I could call her for you." He pointed to number seven where Jane already knew he lived.

The lights were on in the cottage as if someone was home. Jane looked around again, all was quiet but she was sure the spider was watching and waiting.

She was also aware of the dangers of going into a stranger's house and resolved to stay outside whatever happened. Despite the fact the man's presence had halted the spider's attack, Jane felt uncomfortable around him.

She looked him up and down, he had a coat on but it was unzipped. He was wearing rugged outdoor shoes but the laces were untied and just stuffed down the side of each shoe. He had obviously been inside and had come out in a rush. But why would he have done that? She questioned. And if it was because he had heard or seen something from his window, then why hadn't he said so? It was still half a mile to Jane's house and Jane did not want to walk that distance with a giant spider stalking her. So, despite her reservations and the unanswered questions she decided the best option was to take the offer of help.

She had done enough on her own, perhaps if she could convince her mother of what was happening her mother could call the police. It was her only hope of saving Jack. She didn't know where he was, Alfred was not going to help, and danger lurked at every turn. The man was growing impatient in the cold and he checked his watch.

"Yes please, I can give you the number if you don't mind calling for me." Jane replied at last.

"Great, let's go," the man nodded and immediately set off, not waiting for Jane's reply.

Jane followed as he trudged across the road. They drew into the light from the cottage and Jane could see his ankles every time he lifted a leg. He had no socks on and Jane became certain that he had deliberately rushed out from his home and knew more than he was telling. Did he mean to help her? Or, did he have other intentions? Jane wondered. She was not sure and so remained on her guard and trailed behind, just out of his reach. The front door was unlocked, the man walked in and left it open.

Just inside the hall, a traditional corded phone sat on a tall occasional table. The hall was bright and well lit, patterned old-fashioned carpet ran the length of the hall and wallpaper lined the walls. The two clashed horribly with each other and assaulted Jane's eyes. She remained outside on the path; warm musty air rushed out, it had an odour that Jane couldn't place but her nostrils twitched in distaste. The man picked up the phone and stretched out the coiled lead on the handset.

"Right, what's the number?" he asked looking over his shoulder. Jane called the number out and the man tapped it in. She craned to check he had put it in correctly but couldn't quite see the key pad. The man looked back at her. He had the receiver to his ear.

"It's ringing," he said. Jane gave him a grateful half smile. Perhaps it will be okay, she thought. "Ah hello," he said into the mouthpiece. "You don't know me but I am calling on behalf of your daughter, she has asked me to call you." He paused listening to a reply. Jane imagined her mother panicking about her.

"I'm okay," she called out.

"Yes, she's fine," the man placated her mother. "She just needs a lift home that's all, we're at the cottages on Church

Road," he paused again and looked at Jane. "Yes, that's right I live in the orange one, it's number seven. Yes, she's right here. Yes, of course you can speak to her." The man held out the phone to Jane.

Jane shook her head, the lead would not stretch outside and she didn't want to go inside. "I'm sorry. She's outside and quite sensibly doesn't want to come inside into a stranger's house." The man said exactly what Jane had been thinking. He paused listening to her mother and then held out the phone again. He looked genuinely exasperated and was visibly getting frustrated at being used as a go between. "I don't think your mother believes me," he told Jane sounding like he was about to give in. Jane looked around. She didn't relish the thought of walking home.

"My name's Jane and her name is Debbie," Jane said quickly.

"Ah, your name is Debbie and your daughter's name is Jane, she's wearing a woolly beret, a big black coat and she's got a head torch," he listed.

Jane stamped her foot in frustration. Her mother knew Jane didn't have a head torch. Against her better judgement Jane rushed in and took the proffered phone. She untwisted the coiled lead as the man stepped around Jane to allow her to get closer to the phone.

"Mum it's me, can you come and get..." Jane stopped mid-sentence. She could hear the dialling tone in her ear and for a moment she was confused. Then in dread she realised she had been tricked into the cottage. The man had not been speaking to her mum at all and had made the whole conversation up. The gentle click, of the door latch behind her, confirmed her suspicion.

Chapter 14

Jane knew the man had closed the front door and she was trapped inside the house. No one knew she was here, she was no closer to saving Jack and she had no idea what the man wanted with her.

She froze for a moment. The man was behind her, blocking her way to the front door, but he hadn't moved or said anything yet. Perhaps he was sadistically enjoying her discomfort like a cat playing a mouse. She still had her hockey stick in one hand and the phone was in the other.

In front of her at the end of the hall was a closed door, she guessed it went through to the kitchen and perhaps to a back door. To her right were stairs leading up, and to her left was another door. This one was open and Jane could just see a sofa inside. She decided her best chance of escape was through the kitchen, so without turning or saying anything, she dropped the phone, and bolted down the hall towards the closed door.

Jane reached the door at the end of the corridor in a few quick strides. The door had been white once, but time had stained the paint yellow. Hundreds of small pinprick holes peppered the door, except for a large circular area just above Jane's head, evidence that a dartboard had once hung there. Jane grabbed the worn brass handle, and hesitated. She knew she had been quick, but the man had not followed, or said a word.

Her nostrils twitched in warning as they picked up an unsavoury smell, and she gagged slightly. The odour that she had smelt when she entered the house was stronger here. Something didn't seem right, so she turned and looked back down the hall at the man still stood at the front door.

He really was a big man. Tall and overweight, he filled the doorway. He looked at her inquisitively, as if waiting to see what she would do next. Jane was unsure, her hand was still on the door handle, but she hadn't turned it yet. She looked around for inspiration, for a clue as to the man's intentions. Perhaps then, she would know what to do.

Many framed photographs lined the wall. The photograph nearest to Jane was black and white. The frame though, was new, and much larger than necessary. The photograph was creased and warped with neglect, but appeared to have been straightened, and lovingly placed in the centre of the frame. White card filled the frame, and shamed the yellowed paint on the door.

It was a photograph of a family. They were posed in their best clothes, the parents were sat on chairs, and three boys stood with them, two at each side with a hand on the shoulder of each parent, the tallest boy stood at the back in the middle. They were all smiling as if they had just stopped laughing, and the mother beamed in pride and happiness. Her hair was straight and shiny as if it had been recently wet combed, and joy shone out of her eyes.

"My mother," the man said, from the other end of the hall, knowing full well that she would have captured Jane's eye. Jane ignored him, he couldn't be more than forty years old, and the photograph had clearly been taken a long time before he had been born.

The next photograph on the wall was in colour and

featured the man in whose house Jane was trapped. He had his hands cupped in front of him, and in them he held a large brown tarantula-like spider. Its legs were thick in relation to its body, and the whole thing was covered in bushy pale hair. Two thick mandibles hung down from the front of its head, and its black eyes stared out hypnotically from the photograph. Jane's recent experience with a spider was fresh in her mind and she shuddered and looked at the man down the corridor. Her hand tightened on the door handle. The man smiled, and his eyebrows rose, as if he was anticipating something amusing, or about to unwrap a present.

That was enough for Jane and she yanked on the door handle, turned on one foot and shoulder barged the door open. It sprang open easily and banged against the wall. Jane powered forward and looked up just too late.

The stench in the room assaulted her senses, she sucked in a lung full of the thick air and it coated her throat. She tasted it, smelt it, and it stung her eyes. Too late she tried to arrest her run, too late she saw the thick web stretched across the room.

Jane fell forward as she tried to stop and twisted sharply as she did so, to try and stop from falling face first into the web. She ended up falling backwards as if dropping into a trapeze artist's catch net. The web billowed around her and the sticky tendrils caught hold of her and held her fast.

Instinctively she didn't struggle. She had watched flies caught in webs wriggle and struggle until they were completely trapped by the sticky tendrils. She held still and looked back down the hall at the man. He had a look of surprise on his face and then laughed out loud and clapped.

"Brilliant. Brilliant." He laughed. "It never ceases to amaze me how people can get trapped in spider's webs. Hundreds and thousands of years of evolution and here you are, caught in a trap set for something with the intelligence of a fly. Oh dear, dear, dear. You must be truly stupid." He let go of the front door and started to walk down the hall towards Jane. Still clapping and looking smug and spiteful, he clapped the length of the hall. It was a slow mocking clap that matched his expression, and beat out his derision. He was confident and in control, and looked like he was going to savour his moment of power over Jane.

"I don't get many house guests," he said. "Not conscious ones anyway, so when I do, I like to have a little chat. Firstly, just so there is no confusion, this is the end of you." He was totally serious now and looked Jane straight in the eye to convey his seriousness. "I know what happens next and it will be much easier for you if you spend your last moments making peace with yourself. Think about your loved ones. Remember the good times, that sort of thing." He finished and looked for a response from Jane.

Jane's mind was racing. She needed time to work it out, to come up with a way to escape. She was determined that this was not going to be the end of her, as the man had suggested.

"What happens next then?" she challenged, trying to appeal to his spiteful nature.

"Ah well, I'm very glad you asked. You may have noticed that you are in a spider's web. And, given that you ran out of the graveyard in terror, I'm going to assume that you have already met the spider that made it." He paused and looked at Jane to see if she acknowledged his assumption. Jane nodded to keep him going. "Ah good," he said. That should stop you from disbelieving me. It's no fun when people just argue with me. I think it shows a lack of imagination," he smiled, but the smile conveyed no warmth.

Jane wondered how many people had been caught in the web, how many had been lured into the man's house. Did everyone run into it like she had, or did he push them in. He was certainly big enough to manhandle most people.

"Do you know how spiders eat their prey?" he asked.

"I'm not prey," Jane replied firmly, determined not to be a victim.

"Yes, you are, and as I told you before, the sooner you accept your fate the easier it will be for you. Do you know how spiders eat their prey?" he asked his question again, as if interrogating Jane, his voice was firmer and harder this time. She thought perhaps it was wise to reply.

"They suck out the insides," answered Jane and shuddered at the thought.

"No, no, no," said the man. "Everybody thinks that, but spiders don't suck out the insides at all. No, it's much worse than that. First, they bite you and inject you with poison. This won't kill you, but it will paralyse you so that you can't struggle and get away, or hurt the spider. They're delicate creatures you see. Once you are paralysed, the spider will cocoon you and hang you in its web. There you will stay, utterly helpless until the spider gets hungry. If you are lucky you will have died before then, suffocated in the web perhaps, or starved, because that's when it gets really nasty.

When the spider gets hungry and wants to eat, it vomits digestive juices over you. These juices burn and dissolve your skin and your flesh. Of course, if you are still alive you will feel all of this because the poison will have worn off. Once your flesh has dissolved, the spider sucks up the fluid and eats it. Then it vomits more digestive juices onto you and does it again and again until all that is left is your bones and your boots. Oh, and perhaps a little hair, she doesn't like hair. Can you imagine how much that must hurt?" He looked Jane in the eye and raised his eyebrow questioningly.

"You're a monster," spat Jane.

"No, the spider's the monster. I'm merely the friend of the monster. Its carer, if you like." Jane swallowed the fear, and told herself she was okay. She just had to think, nothing was impossible. Her mother always told her that she could achieve anything if she put her mind to it. Well right now she wanted to escape and save Jack.

"Where's my friend?" Jane demanded.

"Why don't you look around," the man replied opening his arms in invitation.

Jane craned her neck around and looked backwards and deeper into the room. She was in a large open plan kitchen that was crisscrossed with webs so thick she couldn't see the back wall. The web was knitted together in sheets that stretched across the room and hung ready to ensnare the unwary.

The kitchen had a flagstone floor and old exposed wooden beams from which a variety of pots, pans, knives and other utensils hung. Some were sharp and threatening, appearing poised ready to drop. The cooking range was old, oil spattered and stained with dried out foodstuffs, a dirty saucepan lay at an awkward angle on the hob with its contents lapping out. The floor, over which Jane lay, was littered with crumbs, and the cracks between the flagstones were filled with decades of spilled fluids and food, congealed into cement that held it all together.

Jane could see animal droppings that lay in runs alongside the walls and cupboards, the mice and rats that patrolled there probably provided the only cleaning the kitchen ever received. Jane could hear them scratching around in the cupboards and she imagined them pouring out in a sea of fur if the cupboard door was opened.

She had a phobia about mice, it was the way mice always knew when they were being looked at and moved into her peripheral vision to remain unseen. They were only ever spotted out of the corner of an eye and they scratched around in the dark spurning the light. Jane shuddered at the thought of being so close to them and looked away from the cupboards and over her shoulder in the other direction.

She gasped in shock as she spotted a string of cocooned bodies dangling from the ceiling. A skeletal arm protruded from the one nearest her. The body twisted in the draught coming through the open kitchen door and turned around to reveal a skeletal head. The eye sockets were black and empty and lank hair hung straight down. The skeleton stank of rotted flesh as the last remnants of the person this once was, putrefied and leaked out onto the floor.

Jane half cried out and half wretched, then lost control of her stomach and bile filled her mouth. She spat it out and turned away from the poor soul hanging in the stinking web filled kitchen, and tried to stretch forward and suck in clean air through the open door. As she moved though the web moved around her and held her fast.

"That's nasty," grimaced the man looking at the bile that Jane had spat on the floor. "Don't they teach you manners at school anymore?" he asked but continued without waiting for a reply. "They wouldn't have stood for that at the orphanage. If I had spat on the floor George Edmund would have had me lick it back up. Not that I would have spat in the first place of course. No, I knew how to behave properly. I was taught manners, I was taught how to conform, and I learnt how to keep my head down and blend in, soon no one even noticed I was there. Soon I just disappeared and everyone forgot about Alfred Thatcher." The name cut through Jane like a knife and she jerked her head up.

"Alfred Thatcher was in the orphanage one hundred years ago. Alfred Thatcher is the brother of Alfred, the shame of Middle Gratestone. You can't be him." Jane refuted his claim to be Alfred Thatcher but at the same time she was recalling the story that Ben Armitage had told at the lunch table.

Could it be possible that Alfred Thatcher had stayed in the orphanage for thirty years? Could it be possible that the man in front of her was over one-hundred-years-old? Could he be the missing brother that had been lost to the poorhouse?

"You know that I am Alfred Thatcher. Don't you?" he said and once again continued without allowing Jane to answer. "I'm quite sure that you didn't believe in giant spiders until tonight. So why is it so difficult to believe that someone just grows older a little slower than other people? I am getting old like everyone else, just in my own time," he smiled, a satisfied self-appreciating smile. "I am Alfred Thatcher and I am one hundred and seven years old." He looked sincere, and spoke with conviction.

Jane was certain from how he spoke that he believed that he was one hundred and seven, but should she believe it as well? He turned to leave and Jane suddenly thought that perhaps it was his presence that was keeping the spider away. She didn't have any clue as to how to escape yet so she spoke quickly to keep him in the room with her.

"Prove it," she fired at him. "Prove that you are Alfred Thatcher," she repeated. The man looked at her and then appeared to relent.

"Why not," he said, I haven't got anything else to do right now. Let me start by telling you the story of my father, Alfred the thatcher.

Alfred half closed his eyes as he thought and began to recite a story that was obviously very familiar to him. He spoke clearly and fluently without hesitation as if he had been there himself. Jane could see that he wasn't lying and that he completely believed in the story he was relating. She focused on what Alfred was saying and pictured the scene he was describing in the hope that she would glean some clue that would help her to escape. Soon they were both totally wrapped up in the story of Alfred the thatcher.

Chapter 15

March 1915

Alfred senior, the thatcher of Middle Gratestone, and father to three sons called Alfred, left home to become Alfred the soldier, and went to fight in the Great War in 1915. He had not wanted to make the transition from artisan to soldier but had felt compelled to do so by the eldest of his three sons. They had opposing views about what should be done about the war and had argued constantly since the war had started.

His eldest son was hot headed and impulsive, he wanted to go to France and fight the Germans. He thought it was his duty and that their family should do their bit. He said the war was justified and if the Government wanted them to fight, and their country needed them to fight, then that was what they must do. The alternative, was to sit at home and let others do the fighting and the dying for them, this would surely bring shame on the family, tarnish their name forever, and at worst, leave their country open to invasion.

Then the war would come to them anyway. Only this time it would affect all their family, Father, Mother and all their sons. The German army would rampage through England and Middle Gratestone and enslave them all. Therefore, the eldest son had said to his father, that as the oldest son he should be the one that went to war. It should be he that stood against the enemy and defended their honour, family and country.

Alfred thought the opposite. They were only one small

family and could not hope to make an impact on the Great War that had Europe in its grip. It would be much better to stay out of it and let the war pass them by. His son was still too young to join the army and Alfred forbade him to do so. However, Alfred knew that his son would be old enough soon and so, to placate him, and prevent him joining up when he could, Alfred realised he had but one choice, he joined the army himself and went to fight to defend their honour, family and country. In this way he hoped that perhaps his son would reconsider, perhaps his son would think that their family had done enough and he would take over responsibility for the family business and stay safe at home.

Alfred worked at the paper factory as a foreman, primarily to keep the worker's cottage that they lived in, but he also ran his own business as a thatcher. He carried out mainly repair work in the winter but in the spring and summer months, after finishing at the factory, he worked in the long balmy evenings replacing whole thatches. He loved the work and had taught his eldest the trade of thatching, and if his eldest followed him to war then there would be no family income at all. Alfred loved all his sons and was certain that this was the only way he had left to prevent his eldest son from joining the army.

It had almost broken his heart when he left home for the last time. His younger sons had not understood why he was leaving them, he could see that. But he couldn't tell them the real reason why he was going to war, then they might blame their older brother, and Alfred didn't want that.

So, he had smiled and pretended it was his idea to go to

war and that it would be a grand adventure and that he would be back home soon. He smiled as much as he could even though inside he felt tragic and bereaved. He had kissed his young sons on the forehead and ruffled their hair as he left, and could still remember the sweet scent of lavender in their hair. Edith had insisted they all be bathed and have their hair washed for his departure. They had run to the photographer's shop in their best clothes in the rain. Edith shone that day and he loved her more than ever.

Alfred was desolate when he left, and as he walked past familiar landmarks to the train station everything he saw reminded him of what he was leaving behind. The field where he had taken Edith for their first picnic together, and years later where he played cricket with his boys on long summer days. They had laughed and cheated each other and had play fights in the grass. The barber shop to where they trooped for their birthday haircuts. Normally Edith would cut the boys' hair, but for their birthdays she insisted they all had a professional haircut. Alfred tried to smile at the memories as he walked on but they only reminded him of how sad he was to leave his family behind. Soon he just stared grimly ahead and tried not to see anything at all.

The mayor, the vicar and the policeman were at the train station to see him off. The eclectic trio fussed over him and wished him well. He was the first person from the town to sign up to fight in the war and the three men congratulated him on his bravery, and slapped him on the back in boisterous encouragement right up until he boarded. Once the train pulled away he glimpsed them again on the platform, not waving but huddled together in conversation and Alfred had an unsettling feeling.

It was some months later that he found himself in France. The army had trained him well and fed him three large meals a day. He was fitter and stronger than he had ever been. He was put in a regiment that had been recruited from the area in which he had lived. He knew many of the men in the regiment from back home and because of that he settled in to army life quickly.

Together they formed a good team and had done well in the few skirmishes that they had had with the enemy. They grew in confidence and Alfred started to think that he might see the war through and return home in victory. He thought all the time about Edith and his boys and longed to see them.

He was shocked though one day in late summer when unexpectedly his eldest son had joined the regiment in France. Alfred had no idea he was coming and Edith had not mentioned it in any of the letters that she had sent. Perhaps she didn't want him to worry, he had thought. He was furious with his son and they had almost come to blows.

His son had explained though that the mayor had persuaded him to go and that the mayor had said that he would ensure that Edith and the boys would be looked after while they both were away. He had passed the family business over to the mayor and gained his assurance that the family would be supported. In the end, father and son had both cried together and agreed that as soon as they could they would return home together. Family was the most important thing and once they had done their bit they would leave the army for good.

One month later, fate intervened and the order was given for an all-out attack on the German lines. Their regiment did well and took some ground, but ammunition ran low and they tired from a lack of water and food, and soon found themselves isolated. The German army counterattack was swift and devastating. Their regiment was overwhelmed and despite extraordinary bravery and intense fighting in which no quarter was asked for and none given. Alfred now found himself sitting in a French field far from home cradling his son's head in his arms.

His son had begged him for help, for him to stop the bleeding somehow, but there was just too much blood. It was coming from everywhere and soaked into the ground and turned the grass red. Alfred watched his son die in front of him and talked to him in kind tones about home and family as he passed on.

All the while as he held his son's gaze, bullets zipped past and plucked at him as the battle raged on. They stung him like angry wasps, but he ignored them and concentrated on his son. By the time the battle moved on, his son was dead, and Alfred was mortally wounded. Tiredness slowly crept up on him as the gloom of evening drew in and his world grew dark. His hand dropped to the floor as his strength left him and he was no longer able to hold his son.

Death had been busy and it was late when Alfred looked up and saw Death approach. Death had seen the worst of man that day, and was full of disgust and revulsion. Wearily Death raised a hand to claim the souls of the father and son, but his hand was stayed by the love that shone from the father's eyes. Love was something that Death had seen very little of that day and it flowed around the two men like a warm summer breeze.

"Take me but save my son," the man begged. Death felt pity for the father and his son but both of their bodies were broken, and so, waved a blackened hand and claimed their souls. With a sigh Alfred crumpled and slipped sideways onto the blood-stained grass and then stood leaving his body behind and together with his son followed Death into the darkness. Death would remember them, and remember the father's request of him.

Chapter 16

"You're speaking about this as if you were there," interrupted Jane. "How can you possibly know what happened?" she asked. The man looked at her.

"I had my own brush with Death," he answered without hesitation. He looked thoughtful now and not threatening at all. "I should have died in the orphanage, I was desperately ill and Death came to me in a dream. Or at least it seemed like a dream. And I think that I was dying, it's quite hard to tell, especially when you're ill because you're not really yourself. Anyway, Death came to me to take my soul, but then hesitated. He showed me how my father and brother had died in France, and how Alfred, the one you know as the shame, died outside the church. He said my father had asked him to save his son, my eldest brother, the Alfred who died with him in the Great War. But Death hadn't been able to because Alfred's body was too badly injured. He couldn't save Alfred outside the church in the snow either because his body was frozen. Death explained to me that he can only take life from one place to another, he can't leave life in a body that won't support it, and he can't make life where there is none. He is a bearer of souls, he takes them from one place to the next and that is all. But I was different. I was dying from a virus, my body could still support life, so Death fulfilled my father's dying wish and finally saved his son by taking the virus and leaving me.

When I woke up I was better. Not only was I better I felt fantastic, I was never ill again, and as I found out in time, I aged much slower than was normal. I am the last Alfred

Thatcher and Death blessed me with long life and good health," he smiled.

"Let me and my friends go then," said Jane. "You don't need us, and we haven't done anything to you." Alfred looked at Jane. The smile that had lingered there slowly disappeared and his mouth straightened and hardened.

"I hate you," he seethed. "You and your kind betrayed us. Look at you, with your jolly hockey stick and smart trendy clothes. You're young and beautiful and you think you own the world. Well you own nothing. You've got your present by stealing my past. Your whole life is built on deceit and lies," Alfred spat out the words in a rage. "You sent us to war, stole our home and our money, you built your own lives using our hard-earned savings. Yes, that's right, my father left money with the mayor to look after us and when he died the mayor put us in the poorhouse and split the money amongst his cronies. The vicar, the baker, the policeman, they were all in on it. They left me to rot in the poorhouse and for thirty years that's what I did. I was always cold, always hungry, always tired. They're things that you and your rich, precious, pampered, privately schooled friends know nothing about, things you've never experienced in your oh so perfect lives. You've lived in luxury with a bed at night to sleep in, and food on the table to eat. I craved food. I still crave it, that's why I overeat. That's why I get wind. I know you've heard me farting in the morning. I bet you've never farted, you disgust me. Well now it's time for you to pay us back. An eye for an eye, a tooth for a tooth, and with the help of Death you and your friends will die and my brother will come back to me.

Alfred isn't dead see, Death didn't take him. He didn't leave him in his frozen body in the snow either, but he didn't take him. He left him here in the statue, not quite dead but not quite alive, so that he might have a chance of life once again. Well the chance has come, it's time to restore the balance. Alfred will live and the descendants of those that wronged us will die." Alfred was red in the face now and was shouting his hatred out at Jane. She recoiled in the face of his fury and looked away, trying not to meet his eye. She realised now she would not be able to reason with him. He was twisted, mad and full of rage. Jane waited for him to calm.

Finally, having vented his anger, Alfred seemed spent and stood up to his full height and straightened his clothing. Then without another word he turned and left, pulling the kitchen door closed behind him.

Jane sighed in relief and looked around for any sign of the spider. There was none but a frantic mumbling sound behind her made her turn a little further. One of the cocoons was wriggling frantically and trying to get Jane's attention. They locked eyes and Jane recognised Ginny's cool light blue eyes shining under long thick eyelashes. She even looks good trussed up in a web, Jane thought to herself. Ginny held Jane's gaze momentarily and then flicked her eyes toward the kitchen door. Her mouth was covered in web and she was unable to speak, but she mumbled behind the gag frantically and nodded at the door.

Jane followed the line of Ginny's eyes towards the door and saw what Ginny had been trying to get her to notice.

On the wall, just an arm's reach from where Jane was lying in the web, was a fire extinguisher. Jane could see the label on it and started to read.

'CO2 (Carbon Dioxide) Fire Extinguisher–for use on liquid and electrical fires. May cause freezing.'

Jane caught on immediately and looked back at Ginny.

"Do you think it will work on the web?" she asked, just loud enough for Ginny to hear, but not so loud that her voice would carry through the door. Ginny nodded and mumbled something incoherent. Jane thought it might have been a swear word. She looked back, slowly rolled over in the web and stretched her arm nearest the extinguisher up towards the clip that held it to the wall mounting. It was tantalising close and Jane pushed with her legs on the floor and stretched as much as the web would allow. Just at the edge of her reach, she managed to hook a finger on the end of the clip. She pulled and the clip popped open and the extinguisher dropped towards the floor. Quickly, Jane thrust out a leg and the extinguisher landed on her foot. Her boot deadened the sound of the extinguisher falling and prevented any injury, but the extinguisher was heavy and Jane stifled a gasp of pain.

Behind her Ginny was mumbling frantically, Jane ignored her and without turning around to look she hooked the extinguisher with her foot and pulled it towards her outstretched hand. As she grabbed it she heard loud music through the door. Alfred had turned up the volume on his speakers, perhaps to drown out any noise that Jane made when the spider returned. It was very convenient for Jane though and she grabbed the extinguisher by the handle and squeezed. Instantly a cloud of white gas jetted out of the extinguisher. Jane turned it towards the web underneath her and enveloped herself in a cloud of gas. The extinguisher hissed loudly and Jane held her breath in the cloud and continued to spray the gas at herself. It was cold through her clothes and freezing on her face. She held the trigger and shook herself violently in the web. With a sudden bump the web, now brittle from the cold, broke and gave up its prize and dropped Jane unceremoniously to the floor. She released the extinguisher trigger, to preserve the gas, and stood up.

Music still throbbed loudly through the door. Jane wondered if Alfred knew something that she didn't. Perhaps the spider came back at the same time every night, and perhaps that time was now. She peered through the sheets of web that laced across the room but couldn't see the spider. Ginny mumbled even louder, she was obviously desperate to be released. So, Jane carefully moved towards her, avoiding the web strands and tried to work out how to release Ginny. Except for her nose and eyes, Ginny was totally cocooned and hanging upside down from a strand of web attached to the ceiling. If Jane fired the extinguisher at the strand attached to the ceiling she would come crashing down but Jane didn't think that she could hold her.

"Hold your breath," she instructed. Ginny sucked in a long breath through her nose and shut her eyes. Jane pulled the trigger and sprayed the gas all around Ginny's upper body. Ginny shook and struggled as they both disappeared in a white cloud.

Jane tried to see through her half-closed eyes, but Ginny

was totally obscured and the gas stung even when Jane opened her eyes just a little. When she thought she had sprayed enough she let go of the trigger, and stood still, holding her breath as the white cloud slowly dispersed. It felt like a long wait, Jane held her breath and squinted out every now and then to check if the gas had cleared. At last Ginny came into view, Jane could see her arms were free and she was quickly brushing off the brittle strands that remained. Jane exhaled and then slowly drew in a lungful of air.

"You can breathe," she said to Ginny. Ginny pulled the web from her face.

"Okay squirt it at my legs I can catch myself in a handstand now." She spoke quietly and urgently but was composed as ever and Jane marvelled at how cool she was. It must have been excruciating for her, hanging upside down in the web, waiting for the spider to return. Jane wondered how long Ginny had been conscious and how much of the conversation with Alfred she had overheard. "Go, go, go," Ginny said and held her breath. Jane did the same and pulled the trigger.

Once again gas enveloped them and obscured the room. Ginny dropped to the floor and knocked into Jane. They both fell backwards and lay there holding their breath as the cloud of gas dispersed once more. Ginny moved first and started brushing the remaining strands of web from her legs. Then she stood and held out a hand for Jane. Jane took the proffered hand and stood up.

"Thank you," said Ginny, looking Jane straight in the eye.

“No problem,” Jane replied. Then they both smiled and hugged. “You’re getting web on me,” Jane remarked kindly and pulled back. “I’m glad you’re okay.”

Chapter 17

"Right we need to get out of here," said Ginny, taking control. Jane didn't mind this time, and if she had to be trapped in a kitchen full of giant spider's web in the house of a mad man then she was glad to be trapped with a resourceful strong girl like Ginny. Jane looked at the mass of web strung across the kitchen, it seemed impenetrable. She could just make out the window at the back, it appeared to be open and must have been how the spider got in and out, however to reach it she and Ginny would have to struggle through the heart of the spider's sticky trap. Tempting as it was to try to fight through it all Jane thought they would simply become ensnared again.

Looking around, Jane counted five cocooned bodies suspended from the ceiling. One was obviously a dog, but the other four were human in shape. Ginny was busy at the kitchen door trying to see underneath it into the hallway beyond.

"The spider got Jack," Jane told her. Ginny looked up.

"He's not here," she said seeing that Jane was looking at the suspended bodies. "All those bodies in the web are old and long dead. There's another spider as well as this one though. One caught me and brought me here, another caught my mum. I don't know where it took her but perhaps it took Jack as well and they're in the same place. I was out of it for a while, I think they might have been brought here first. There were lots of comings and goings," Ginny offered Jane in explanation. Jane nodded sadly.

"I'm sorry about your mum," she apologised. Ginny

acknowledged Jane with a curt nod, Jane could see she was worried. "I think I might know where they are," Jane said. "We were sharing stories today and Lottie Barnes thought she might have seen a giant spider in the church tower. We should try there." Jane was desperate to find Jack and hoped Ginny would help her.

"Okay," agreed Ginny without hesitation. "I think we need to go out the front, do you want the extinguisher, or can I have my hockey stick back?" she asked Jane with a smile.

"I'm getting used to the weight now," replied Jane balancing the hockey stick in her palm. "The balance is a little bit off centre, but it's not too bad. I'll keep the stick thank you," she continued. Ginny was already reaching for the extinguisher.

"I knew you would say that," she said grabbing the extinguisher. "And it only feels off balance because you're so puny," she mocked in good humour. The girls gathered by the door, Jane gripped the hockey stick tightly and nodded her readiness to Ginny.

Ginny had the extinguisher in one hand and slowly turned the door handle with the other. The music was still blaring out and it increased in volume as Ginny opened the door. Jane stepped into the hallway. It was clear. She could see the lounge door had been closed and the music was coming from inside. She guessed that despite Alfred's hatred for her he still didn't have the stomach for blood. Perhaps he was in there trying to pretend that she wasn't being consumed by a giant spider. Somehow trying to shed himself of the guilt that maybe he was feeling in what little humanity he had left. Ginny pressed a hand in Jane's back to urge her forward, and Jane moved on quickly and quietly into the hall.

She paused at the phone; Ginny stepped past her and started to pull bolts and locks on the front door. Jane lifted the receiver, there was a dialling tone so she pressed nine-nine-nine and dropped the receiver to the floor. Ginny pulled the door open and without saying anything they stepped out into the cold and closed the door behind them. The curtains on the front window were closed, so the girls edged up the garden path trying unsuccessfully to walk quietly in the icy snow. It crunched alarmingly loudly and the girls grimaced needlessly. Once in the road they scurried across to the church gate and paused there.

"My mobile phone is in my mum's car," said Ginny. "We can call the police and get help," she went to leave, but Jane grabbed her shoulder and hauled her back.

"Not a good idea I'm afraid," Jane said. "It's not just spiders that are out there tonight. I got attacked by a giant fox creature earlier. I know it doesn't sound scary but it was massive. I ran to your car and managed to trap it inside. I left it in there, so if your phone is in there, then it's out of reach for now." Jane looked at Ginny wondering if Ginny would believe her, or be angry, or still want to go and get the phone anyway. Jane really didn't want to have to face that creature again.

"My mum will be furious if it chews up her Louis Vuitton bag," Ginny responded and then continued unperturbed. "Your mum doesn't let you have a mobile phone, does she?" she asked Jane, already knowing full well that Jane was not allowed one.

Jane shook her head. Her dad had given her a phone once, but she had managed to rack up an enormous bill in the first month, and so it had been confiscated and she had been without ever since.

"No, my dad says I'm not responsible enough," Jane complained.

"He's got that right." Ginny quipped.

"Apparently, I became unable to communicate with anyone unless an electrical interface was involved," Jane continued ignoring the quip for now. "Dad said I only conversed with people that were in a different room to me, and as soon as that person was in the same room then I ignored them and started conversing with someone else that wasn't in the same room. He doesn't get it though, obviously I don't need to tell anyone in the same room as me where I am and what I am doing, they already know. And I don't need to find out what they're doing because I can see what they are doing. I only need to communicate with people that I can't see. It's obvious, isn't it? Anyway, I don't have a phone now, you are correct. And in response to your last statement, I saved you, didn't I?" Jane finally retorted.

"And I suppose you are never going to let me forget it." Ginny smiled.

"I'm going to remind you every day for the rest of your life," affirmed Jane. "If we get through tonight," she added under her breath, and then thought for a moment. "There's something else as well," she warned, and held Ginny's wrist to convey her seriousness. Ginny caught the tone in Jane's voice, and looked her in the eye in the dim light. Jane decided there was no other way of saying it, other than coming straight out with her theory. "I think Mr Spinner is the spider and Mr Cunningham is the fox," she blurted. "I don't know who the other spider is, and I don't know if there are more of them," she finished.

"Right," replied Ginny taking a moment to think. "Let's go find Jack and my mum. We're right next to the church anyway so...can't leave without checking the tower," she said grimly. They both looked towards the church door at the end of the path, nervous about what lay ahead, but pumped up after their escape from number seven Church Road, and took stock of their situation.

It was late, the organ music had stopped and most of the church lights were off. The large stained-glass windows that adorned the church and earlier had shone in glorious colour were now dark and sinister, the pious figures depicted on the window that had danced and sung together before, now appeared indistinct and huddled in secret collusion. They're up to no good, thought Jane irrationally.

"Come on," said Ginny and opened the gate. She seemed unaffected by the threatening setting and Jane wondered whether Ginny was truly fearless, or whether she was so single minded she was oblivious to everything but her ultimate goal. Before following Ginny down the path, Jane hesitated and looked back at Alfred Thatcher's cottage. The door and curtains were still closed, and the thick walls and curtains reduced the sound of his music to a faint tinny tapping. Satisfied that their escape had gone unnoticed Jane followed Ginny to the large iron bound church door.

In typical Ginny style, Ginny walked straight up to the door and turned the door handle. It turned easily so she planted her legs and pushed the door firmly open. As it opened she became faintly silhouetted in the doorway by the few lights that remained on in the church. Jane looked over Ginny's shoulder and they both peered into the gloom as the large door creaked and groaned open.

The church was rectangular. The tower was offset on the left about halfway down the building. The doorway they stood in was at one end of the nave and they could see down the entire length of the church. It was filled with church pews running either side of a central walkway. Grand ornate pillars supported the high arched roof and lined the way to the altar that was stood on a raised stone platform at the end and decked in red and patterned in gold. A lofty pulpit projected out over the altar, and numerous alcoves and doors that led to small side rooms, provided shadowed hiding places.

Candles lit up the altar and flickered in the draught from the open door causing the shadows to move and dance. The organ music had stopped and the creaking door echoed loudly in the interior as it completed its ponderous journey to the side wall. Jane looked to the pipe organ behind the altar, the organist's seat and the choir pews were set slightly lower than the altar, and as such were obscured. A light was on in a side room at the far end, and Jane wondered if whoever had been playing the organ was still inside.

Ginny stepped in and pulled the door back slightly to

check there was nobody or nothing hiding behind it. Once Jane was inside, Ginny walked the door slowly closed in a long sweeping arc, and pushed it hard against the frame, so that the lock latched in place. It clicked loudly with a sense of finality as if the last nail had just been hammered into their coffins.

Chapter 18

"Which service?" asked the telephone operator promptly in a cool efficient voice and waited for a reply from the caller. The caller didn't respond so the operator repeated the question. "Which service?" she asked, speaking a little louder and annunciating her words clearly. Normally by now whoever had dialled nine-nine-nine to report an emergency would be breathlessly and urgently asking for either the police, fire or ambulance service. However, on this occasion the caller remained quiet. The operator listened, she could clearly hear some form of classical music being played loudly in the background, but other than that she could not hear anything that would indicate the nature of the emergency. She looked at the monitor sat on her desk, it displayed the phone number and address that the call had been made from.

It was a house phone in Middle Gratestone at number seven Church Road. She noted the time, it was getting late now and perhaps it was unlikely to be a young child playing with the buttons and inadvertently dialling nine-nine-nine. Young children often gave themselves away by continuing to press buttons after getting through and playing out tell-tale beeps to the operator. So, discarding that possibility and without any further delay she forwarded the call to the police.

The police emergency response operator received the call and checked his monitor. The call had been logged as a potential hoax call. He listened to the music being played in the background for a short while before speaking, it was important that he made the right decision. It could be a hoax, or it could be that the person calling was under duress or unable to speak.

"Police, what is the nature of your emergency?" he asked. The sound of violins playing was all he received in reply. He looked again at his monitor, there was only one resident registered at the address and he was a forty-five-year-old male, he was not registered on the database as having difficulty speaking on the phone and he was not the normal age of someone that would make a hoax call. That left the possibility that perhaps the person calling was incapacitated in some way or even under duress or coercion. So, without delay he decided further investigation was required and forwarded the call to the police force responsible.

The police officer at the control desk in Middle Gratestone police station was very interested in the information that was passed to him by the emergency response operator. It was invariably quiet at night and he had just ordered pizza when he received his first call about an hour earlier. He now had several reports from members of the public in Middle Gratestone that warranted further investigation and he was about to dispatch a car.

There were two separate missing person reports, one had been reported by a worried husband that his wife and daughter had not returned home and would not answer his calls to their mobile phones, and another one from an anxious mother whose daughter had not come back from school that evening. He also had a report of a large dog loose in the area. This latest report, of a possible hoax or person under duress call, was in the same area as all the other reports and so he decided that it gave him an exact location to where to send the police car first and he dispatched it immediately.

Henry Rogers was Jack's father and a policeman. He had left Middle Gratestone to join the Metropolitan Police Force as a young man but had returned once his thirst for adventure had been sated and now much preferred the gentler country beat. He came from a long line of policeman and had always been expected to follow in his father's footsteps. Strong, professional and streetwise he prided himself on maintaining the peace in his home town. He had had very little serious crime to deal with in his 15 years on the beat in Middle Gratestone but his early years in the 'Met' had instilled in him a cautious wary approach that had served him well.

As such he completed a slow drive down Church Road before turning the police car around and parking outside number three just down from number seven and out of direct view of the front windows of the cottage. He used the car radio to inform control he had arrived.

The street seemed quiet. There were no street lamps out here towards the edge of town. But light from the cottages found chinks in the closed doors and curtains and leaked out, dimly lighting the road and picking out footprints in the snow from the day's comings and goings. Henry walked slowly down the centre of the road, there was no traffic and no people in sight out on the street, even the hardiest teenagers were inside staying warm.

There were footprints in and out of number seven and

lights were on behind the thick curtains. Henry could hear tinny music coming from within, and he paused just off the property to try to appraise the situation. A tendril of smoke stretched out from the chimney reaching to the dark sky. Henry observed that the occupant had clearly been inside long enough to get a wood fire going.

"PC542, Control anything more on Church Road?" he asked speaking into the radio microphone attached to the shoulder of his stab vest.

"Control, negative Henry," control replied ignoring radio procedure and using Henry's name in an attempt to ruffle Henry's feathers. Henry's colleagues often deliberately disregarded protocol because despite the fact Henry had been at the station for 15 years, he was still ribbed for being the big shot from the city who knew all the rules and regulations. His colleagues thought it amusing to attempt to get Henry to quote the regulation they had just transgressed. Henry knew the lads at the station each kept score cards and competed to get the most quotes from him. He didn't mind joining in though and tried to quote the more obscure regulations whenever possible.

Tonight though, Henry ignored the obvious regulation transgression because something deep in the pit of his stomach was gnawing at him, warning him to keep focused and stay on task. His sixth sense jangled in noisy alarm and he looked around warily, something was wrong.

Henry walked slowly towards the front door continuing to look around as he did so and pressed the bell push next to the door. It rang loudly and Henry kept his finger on the bell push for just too long and then took a couple of steps back away from the door so he could observe the curtains. The music stopped and sure enough a moment later the curtains twitched and a crack of light lanced out. Henry nodded in the direction of the opened curtain to let the occupant know that he had seen them, and waited where he was just back from the door.

People generally opened their doors to the police in Middle Gratestone, and if they had looked out of a window first and then knew it was the police, they rushed to do so, expecting bad news about a relative or someone else. They were never concerned about themselves or worried about being arrested because invariably they had done nothing wrong. This was a law-abiding town in which everyone looked out for everyone else and in which people followed the rules. So, Henry waited patiently a couple of steps back from the door expecting it to be opened immediately.

Inside the cottage after peeking through the curtain and seeing a policeman at his door, Alfred opened the lounge door and tiptoed quietly to the closed kitchen door, he opened it slowly, ever wary of the spider that lived within, and surveyed the scene without turning on the kitchen light. The baker's daughter was gone, the web she had been held in was torn and hanging in shreds, and looking further back he could see that the recently cocooned tall blonde girl was gone as well. Dumbfounded for a moment, he looked around and saw the open clamp on the wall which until recently had held the fire extinguisher.

"Clever girls," he mumbled, realising what they had done. He was worried now, there was only one policeman outside and perhaps with the element of surprise Alfred could overpower him, but what had the girls reported to the police? And how did the policeman get here so quick? There had only been time for a couple of tracks to play in the lounge since he had left the kitchen.

He thought quickly, surely the police wouldn't listen to any stories about giant spiders and the girl's claims would be dismissed as a hoax. Perhaps this was why the police were not smashing his door down and arresting him. It seemed more like an investigatory visit than a planned arrest and so Alfred decided to answer the door. He looked down the hall and could see the chain was off the door and the deadlocks had been pulled, he knew he had locked them before going into the lounge so assumed the girls had left by the front door.

He also noticed the phone was dangling down from the table, the coiled cord was stretched out straight and the handset just touched the floor as if it was reaching up to the table. He walked over and picked it up.

"Hello," he spoke into the handset.

"Police emergency, are you in need of assistance?" the operator immediately answered.

"No," Alfred replied. "I'm fine," he added speaking deadpan trying not to sound tense or worried.

"Is there anyone else there that may need help or assistance?" the operator pressed on trying to ascertain the reason for the emergency call.

"No," Alfred replied. "The nine button sticks on my phone, I think I may have accidentally phoned nine-nine-nine by mistake," he added trying to pre-empt the operator's next question and hoping that his weak explanation was sufficient to allay the operator's concerns.

"Sir, can you confirm your name, address and date of birth?" the operator asked. Alfred thought he was about to be caught out by the operator and decided he might have a better chance of convincing the policeman that there was nothing untoward happening and that no assistance was required.

"There's a policeman outside on my doorstep, I'm going to let him in, thank you for your concern but I do not need any assistance, goodbye."

Alfred hung up the phone and then turned to the front door. He kept a heavy wooden walking stick behind the door. It was gnarled and knotted and was topped with a large fist-sized lump of wood that served as a handle. He didn't use it to walk and had specifically bought it as a weapon that he could keep at the front door propped inconspicuously in the corner with his umbrella. He took hold of the stick and then opened the door, just a crack, so that he could see through, and placed his foot behind it so that it could not be readily barged open.

Alfred looked the policeman up and down. He was tall and well-built and was dressed in full police gear including a protective anti-stab vest. He had a hat pulled down just over his eyes that shaded them and prevented Alfred from reading him. His face was lean, fit looking and weather worn from many years on the beat. He had a tough, confident look and stared back at Alfred from under the peak, unsmiling and stern.

Alfred though was from the orphanage, he was used to looking after himself and was not easily intimidated.

“Yes?” he said to the policeman outside, in confrontation rather than welcome.

By the time Alfred answered the door Henry was deeply suspicious that something criminal was going on. Alfred’s curt unfriendly welcome and obvious reluctance to speak to him confirmed his suspicions.

“Constable Rogers from Middle Gratestone police station,” Henry informed Alfred “We have received an emergency call from this address can I be of assistance?” Henry asked politely.

“No, I’ve just explained to your operator that the nine button sticks on my phone and I must have inadvertently dialled nine-nine-nine. There is no emergency and nobody here needs assistance. I’m very sorry to have wasted your time it was not my intention to do so,” Alfred lied quickly and fluently as if he had spent his whole life doing so.

Henry nodded in understanding to try and show some empathy with Alfred’s explanation and then continued.

“Are you the owner of the property?” he asked. “Could anyone else have dialled nine-nine-nine?” he questioned offering Alfred a possible explanation.

“No, I’m alone, I told you it was an accident, now will that be all I’m very busy,” Alfred snapped as he started to lose patience and his cool with it. Henry looked at him for a moment and then got out his notebook from his pocket and carefully opened it up.

“Are you Alfred Thatcher?” he asked.

“Yes, I am,” snapped Alfred. Henry pulled out a short pencil sharpened at both ends.

“Yes, I am,” he repeated out loud as he wrote. Henry

put the pencil and notepad away and then took a step towards the cracked open door to better see Alfred's face. "We're looking for some missing school children. They would have passed by this way. Have you seen them?" he asked, looking Alfred straight in the eye.

Alfred was taken aback by the sudden direct questioning and was flustered for a moment. The policeman's eyes were suddenly visible in the light from the open door and they were cold blue in colour and hard. Alfred realised the policeman would not be brushed off easily and gripped the heavy walking stick a little tighter.

"Perhaps they are playing hockey or something," he answered, picturing Jane with her hockey stick.

"Yes, perhaps," agreed Henry. "I must remind you that it is against the law to waste police time and I shall have to file a report at the station, it is procedure you understand. You may receive a letter explaining the laws you have broken and possibly making further requirements of you such as presenting yourself at the police station or requiring you to attend court. Thank you, have a good evening." Henry turned to leave and then turned back. "Perhaps you could get someone to take a look at that phone. I'm sure you don't want to waste more police time." He turned and walked back down the garden path without waiting for Alfred's reply.

Alfred watched him go and wondered if he had been sufficiently convincing or if the policeman suspected something. Had the policeman remained any longer, Alfred was sure that he would have had to use his stick and attack him. Deep in thought, he closed the front door, turned and leant back on it and let out a deep sigh. He had known for a long time that tonight would be a tense night and that the plan that he and his brother had decided on was fraught with difficulty, but until now he hadn't realised how difficult it would be. The police being involved so early was an unexpected problem. The spiders were meant to catch the two girls and the boy, his brother controlled the spiders and they were out there doing his bidding. But the girls weren't meant to escape and they certainly weren't meant to bring the police down on him as well.

Alfred smiled out of relief, at least he wasn't in a prison cell, and then he held his smile as his emotions changed to satisfied spite and he broke out into a laugh. He knew the policeman. He had known him as soon as he had seen him outside. He was the policeman Henry Rogers, father to Jack Rogers and son of another Henry Rogers. A long line of policeman ran in their family, right back to the Rogers that had conspired to throw the two young Alfred Thatcher brothers out on the street, and Henry, the boy that had punched Alfred's brother to the ground outside the church one hundred years ago. And he knew those two little rich brats. One was descended from Mr Rose the baker, that wouldn't give a loaf of bread to a starving boy, and the other was descended from the mayor, that had encouraged his father and brother to go to war and then hidden the Thatcher family money, and finally written down a pack of lies in the account of what happened to their family in the town records.

Well tonight he and Alfred would have their revenge. By morning his brother Alfred would be returned to him, alive once again, and one of those kids, either one of the girls, or the boy–he really didn't care which–would be dead. Nothing was going to stop them tonight, not those kids, and not one nosey policeman. Alfred laughed out loud for no one's benefit but his own and then returned to his lounge, still chuckling, and put his music back on. He had about an hour to wait until he needed to be back at the statue, so he sat down and put his feet up to relax.

Henry walked back to the police car and got inside, pulling the door quietly closed behind him. He thought for a moment and then spoke into the car radio.

"PC542 to Control, Alfred Thatcher is up to something but I don't know what yet, he's definitely seen the girls at some point tonight so I'm going to stay here and watch his house for a while." There was a pause and then the speaker in the car burst into life.

"Control, roger that, no further info on the girls this end," Control replied. Henry sat in the dark watching the cottage from the car, and pondered.

He hadn't told Alfred Thatcher that it was two girls that were missing, Henry knew both Jane and Ginny well, they were friendly with his son and it wasn't like either of them to be missing. Both girls were hockey mad and Henry did not believe that it was by coincidence that Alfred Thatcher had mentioned hockey.

Why would Alfred assume that the missing children were going to play hockey unless he had seen them? Why not football or rugby? Why hockey?

Henry was certain. Alfred Thatcher had seen the girls that night and he knew where they were. So, from now on, for the rest of the night, Henry was going to be Alfred's shadow, and Alfred was going to lead him right to them.

"Right then Alfred, let's see what you're up to," Henry said starting the car and putting the headlights on.

He pulled out slowly and then drove past the house. If Alfred was still watching, Henry wanted him to see the car leave and think that he had got away with whatever he was up to. At the end of Church Road, he turned right towards the school, and once out of view turned off the car lights and pulled over. As he slowed to a halt he could see a car on the other side of the road, it was parked half on and half off the verge and looked out of place. He recognised it instantly as the same type and colour of car that Ginny's mother drove, and Ginny and her mother had both been reported as missing. The windows were all steamed up, as if somebody was inside, and Henry decided that before he returned on foot to keep a watch on Alfred Thatcher's house that he should take a quick look at the car...

Chapter 19

Inside the church, both girls stood quietly and took in their surroundings, scanning around and listening intently for any sign of danger. The church was typical of all old English churches, its walls were built from solid stone blocks, and the arched ceiling high above, was decorated in complicated murals and supported by ornate beams that ended in carved angels. Stone slabs, engraved with the names and dates of long forgotten history, paved the floor on which the girls stood. The slabs were worn and uneven, scuffed smooth by centuries of churchgoers walking over the long dead dignitaries and friends of the church that were entombed beneath them.

Lists of the dead from two world wars were engraved into stone plaques on the wall and a statue of Christ dying on the cross was mounted halfway down, high on the wall opposite the pulpit, to be visible from everywhere in the nave. Images of death surrounded Jane and Ginny, and this building of joyful worship during the day, now only served to remind them of the danger they were in and of their own fragile mortality.

Jane was unsure what to do next. Perhaps they should look for whoever it was that was still here and enlist their help. Or perhaps they should sneak quietly to the tower and free Jack without anyone noticing.

“What shall we do?” she deferred to Ginny. In doing so she had a sudden realisation and a fog that had clouded her vision for a long time cleared. As she asked the question something occurred to Jane, something that perhaps she had always known.

She realised that her long dislike of Ginny had been down to jealousy. Ginny had done nothing but be brilliant and beautiful and Jane had been jealous of her. Here though in the face of danger Jane deferred to Ginny's fearless brilliance and was grateful for her presence, but at school, especially where Jack was concerned, Jane had challenged Ginny at every turn and in doing so had eroded their friendship. She warmed to Ginny now and touched her arm. "I'm glad you're here," she told Ginny in acknowledgement of all the wrongs she had committed against her.

"Me too," replied Ginny simply. "Now let's find Jack and my mum and get out of here."

The girls smiled at each other and then spread out a little, Ginny took one side of the main aisle and Jane the other. Together they started to slowly walk towards the altar. Jane gripped the hockey stick across her body ready to use it in defence as a shield rather than swing it in attack. Ginny paced forward silently in a slight crouch swinging left and right as she walked aiming the extinguisher into the shadows. Halfway down they stopped and stood still in the main aisle in line with the door that led to the tower. It was another large iron bound door like the main door to the church they had just entered through. As they approached they could see there was no light visible coming under it, so Jane cocked an ear and listened for a moment. Ginny stood quietly by her side and then broke the silence rather curtly.

"Let's just go for it," she declared impatiently. Jane looked at Ginny, she realised that Ginny wanted to push on whatever the danger to get to her mum and Jack as quickly as possible. It was a curse of the confident to be impatient and rash and Jane felt a softer more measured approach was probably wiser, however in the absence of a better suggestion of her own she nodded and reached for the door handle.

It turned and she pulled the heavy door open, giving it a hard tug so that it gained momentum, and then let it go and stood back. It swung open silently and slowed to a neat stop just before it hit the wall. The room that the open door revealed was unlit and gloomy, the walls were uncovered, and the large dark stone, from which the tower was built, darkened the room even more and created impenetrable blackness in the corners.

Jane could see the lower ends of the colourful church bell ropes dangling down in the centre of the room, they were still and undisturbed, and behind them a wooden staircase led upwards from the far wall. A faint far off musty smell slowly wafted out and Jane recognised the smell from Alfred Thatcher's kitchen. It was the smell of putrid decay and thick sticky web. Jane realised that there must be bodies in the tower, cocooned like before, in a spider's twisted layered trap and left hanging like carcasses in a butcher's freezer.

Her mind started to race. She took a step forward to peer around the door jamb into the corners of the room nearest to the door. As she did so and as the smell filled her nostrils the truth ambushed her. A giant spider could not have remained in the tower undiscovered. Someone must know that the spider had a web here and that there were bodies in the tower. And it couldn't just be Alfred Thatcher, it must also be someone who worked here in the church. Perhaps even everyone that worked in the church.

"The vicar must be involved," she said out loud. Ginny shushed her from behind, and at the same moment something wet dripped onto the top of Jane's forehead.

Startled, she turned and looked up, raising her hockey stick in defence and looked straight into a bank of black bottomless eyes under which a pair of glistening fangs dripped wet mucus. The spider's front legs whipped out and made a grab for Jane but she was already ducking and with a shriek dived back through the doorway. The spider was quick though and it dropped and twisted through the doorway, its eight legs scratching on the walls and floor as it did so and it was instantly on top of Jane again. Jane tried to hold back the fangs with the hockey stick but the spider was too strong. The fangs extended out ready to plunge into Jane and inject the paralysing poison.

Then just as Jane braced herself ready to feel the fangs sink into her flesh, they disappeared in a freezing white cloud of gas from the extinguisher. The spider's weight came off Jane and she scrambled backwards holding her breath until she was out of the cloud.

"Come on," said Ginny emerging from the cloud and hauling Jane to her feet. Together they ran for the altar and ducked behind it. Jane remained hidden for an agonising second or two as she caught her breath and then she had to look. She peeked over the top of the altar, past the silver candelabra that held the burning candles, and watched. The thick cloudy gas hung in the air and slowly thinned. As it cleared the spider stepped forward and emerged into the flickering candle light.

The spider was a fearsome creature and for the first time Jane got a clear view of it. It stood on eight thick black legs armoured in black jointed plates and protected by thick thorn like bristles. Its body was bloated, and covered in black hair, patched here and there, by brown raised clumps. It had two large black eyes in the centre of its head and another pair of smaller eyes each side. There was no pupil that Jane could see and the eyes shone like black glass reflecting the flickering candle light back at her. Underneath the eyes, two fangs dripped mucus that Jane guessed was the poison it used to paralyse its victims.

The spider moved slowly forward out of the cloud, treading carefully and purposefully, straight towards Jane and Ginny. Ginny fired off the extinguisher again and shouted aggressively trying to warn off the advancing creature. It stopped about ten yards from the altar and watched them impassively.

"We can't stay here," Jane said to Ginny, her voice was panicked after her brush with the spider and she found herself drawn by the black eyes and the flames that swayed hypnotically in them. The altar in front of her offered little protection and while the fire extinguisher was certainly proving effective it wasn't going to last all night.

"Right," replied Ginny, her voice was calmer than Jane's but anxious nonetheless. "Okay," she continued, trying to think of a way out. "Okay, I'll fire the last of the extinguisher at it then we run to the side wall, turn left and down to the tower doorway. Once inside we can close the door and lock the spider in here." She didn't sound convinced though and Jane looked across at her.

Ginny was clearly agitated and Jane remembered that Ginny had already been attacked and caught by the spider once already. She suspected that Ginny was about to react, and on past record she would probably react impulsively and aggressively. Jane pictured Ginny running at the spider screaming and firing the extinguisher as she went, and heroic as the image was, she thought that despite all Ginny's bravery she would not come off the better.

Then Jane remembered the sockets that she had in her pocket, she pulled one out and moved away from Ginny and the altar to get a clear swing. As Ginny watched curiously Jane lobbed the socket in the air and in one fluid movement swung the hockey stick. It connected cleanly with the socket as it dropped and fired it straight at the spider that had started to advance slowly forward again as if it was stalking the two girls. The socket struck the spider on an armour plate on one of its legs and ricocheted off with a crack that was satisfying to the girls and alarming to the spider.

"Good shot!" congratulated Ginny as the spider scuttled to one side.

Jane produced another socket and fired that one at the spider as well which was now steadily backing off. The second socket skimmed underneath the spider, missing its legs but nicking the spider's abdomen and deflecting to the stone floor where it bounced and then clattered around the pews. Although its impassive eyes were expressionless its body seemed to jerk up and down for a moment and both girls were certain it had been stung by the shot.

"Give it another one," encouraged Ginny, feeling that for once they seemed to have the upper hand.

Jane fired another socket at the creature, once again it whistled under the spider but this time bounced off one of its hind legs.

"Right let's run for it," shouted Ginny preparing to make a dash for the tower door. As she spoke the spider sprang into action as if it had understood what Ginny had said. It scuttled across to the wall by the tower door and then, without stopping, started to climb. Its feet gripped easily on the hewn rock and without slowing it scuttled up the wall as if it were still on level ground. The girls watched its progress in silent admiration at its adept skill as it left the wall and crossed the ceiling to the centre of the nave. Ginny grabbed Jane's arm.

"Let's go now," she said, sensing that they had an opportunity.

The girls rounded the table and rushed for the door but the spider was quicker, it dropped from the ceiling like a stone, to block their path and then hung suspended just off the ground from a thin strand of web. It swung gently and the girls stopped and backed up until they were behind the altar once more. From there they watched the spider at work. It dropped to the ground and then scuttled to the opposite wall and attached the web so that it stretched from the ceiling to the wall. It then repeated the process but this time attached the strand to the other wall.

"It's building a web to trap us in here," Jane guessed. "The longer we stay here the thicker that will be and the less chance we have of getting out of here, we've got to go now!" Jane said agreeing Ginny's plan. "I'll fire a couple of the spanner things at it, you fire off the extinguisher and we run for the tower like you said," Jane looked at Ginny for confirmation. Ginny smiled, and then nodded.

"Okay, agreed let's do it," she affirmed and raised the extinguisher. Jane took a step back and prepared to lob a socket in the air and smash it with the hockey stick at the spider, as it scuttled across in front of her still busying itself constructing a web.

"You won't make it," said a voice from behind her. Jane jumped and the spider stopped and took a hesitant step backwards as it appraised the new arrival. Jane froze in disbelief for a moment and then looked back, she recognised the voice and sure enough there behind her was her classmate David, the vicar's son. David walked up to the two girls from the back of the church and stood between them behind the altar. "It's too quick, and it knows you'll try to get to the tower door. It's actually quite clever and it knows what you're saying," David explained.

He was dressed casually in jeans, sweatshirt and trainers, his hair was messy and he looked worried and anguished.

"You shouldn't have come here," he continued and looked sideways at Jane. "Why didn't you listen to all my stories. They were meant to warn you off. I tried Jane I really tried to stop you coming here. I told you those stories to keep you away, not to bring you in. I know you're scared of the statue already. Why did you come?" He asked imploringly as his eyes searched Jane's for an answer.

Although Jane hadn't moved she was thinking fast, and

keeping an eye on the spider which seemed to have been put off by David. It was obvious that David had seen the spider before and had known about it for a while.

"Why were you trying to stop me coming here?" Jane demanded, feeling betrayed by her friend.

"It's complicated Jane, but tonight, Alfred, the shame of Middle Gratestone, is going to be brought back that will free my dad from his curse and everything can get back to normal again," David replied.

"How will it free your dad? How will Alfred be brought back?" demanded Ginny still pointing the fire extinguisher at the spider. David looked down at the floor and then away. There were tears appearing in his eyes and he was struggling to speak. Finally, he blurted it out.

"One of you will take Alfred's place," David said in an explosion of emotion. His face crumpled and the tears came fast. "I'm sorry," he apologised. "It's not my fault I didn't know what to do, I just didn't want it to be you," David looked directly at Jane and carried on talking in a rush as if he had waited a long time to say all this and now couldn't get it out quick enough. "They want someone descended from the people that they believe were responsible for Alfred's death, and I didn't want it to be you Jane so I tried to scare you off. Please forgive me." David finished his confession and looked at Jane hoping for forgiveness but not expecting any.

Jane felt sorry for David and was about to speak when Ginny butted in.

"So, if I have understood this correctly you didn't want it to be Jane, but you were more than happy for it to be me."

Ginny's voice was steeped in anger; Jane didn't have to look at her to know how angry she was. "Or my mother, or Jack, you were more than happy for it to be them," Ginny's voice rose in pitch. "That's it, I'm going to smash this spider and then I'm going to smash you," there was steel in her voice now.

"No," jumped in David. "The spider is my dad, the statue's controlling him, he doesn't know what he's doing," David was losing it and tears were rolling down his cheeks. "I'm sorry okay," he said moving sideways away from the girls and around the altar. "I couldn't stop it, and I can't take it back, but maybe I can make it up to you." David rounded the table and started to back towards the spider. "You want to get to the tower, right?" he questioned and then provided the answer before Jane or Ginny could respond. "Perhaps I can give you the time that you need." David continued walking slowly backwards and stretched out his arms, he was close to the spider now. "I'm sorry Jane," David said and closed his eyes as he continued backwards right up to the spider.

Jane shook her head and mouthed 'no' as the spider's head reared and then snapped back down. Its fangs pierced David's body and sank deep into his shoulder. David's eyes opened wide in pain and he reached back and clawed at his back for a moment, as if fear and hurt had changed his mind and dashed his conviction, then his knees buckled and his body went limp. The spider caught him before he hit the ground with its two front legs and started to roll him on his side like a spindle just above the floor. Web came fast from the spinnerets under the spider's body and it started to cocoon him in sticky web. Ginny grabbed Jane.

"Come on," she said urgently and pulled at Jane. "We've got to go or we're next," she implored.

Jane plunged back into reality, she had been transfixed by the spider slowly turning David in its grasp, and Ginny's words brought her out of it. The girls ran to the side wall as Ginny had planned earlier and then back to the tower door. It was still open so they rushed in together and slammed it shut behind them leaving David and the spider trapped in the nave.

"Oh my God, oh my God," repeated Jane, fumbling in her pocket for the head torch and turning it on. "What if it eats him?" she said to herself, more than to Ginny.

Ginny stood in front of Jane and placed a hand on her shoulder, while Jane flashed the torch around checking all the nooks and crannies in the tower.

"It was cocooning him like it did to me before," Ginny told her. "He'll be okay for now. Not that he deserves to be." There was a little tenderness in Ginny's voice now, she was sensitive to Jane's feelings, and although anger at David still fired her she could not discount his sacrifice. "Look," she said. "He's given us a chance, let's not waste it. We need to save Jack and we need to save my mum. Perhaps we can also stop whatever it is that is going on as well. Because I don't think that bringing someone back from the dead is going to result in anything good."

Jane nodded, she knew Ginny was right. They had to see this through, Jane had been trying to help Jack for hours, and what she needed now, so that she could keep going, was to find that commitment that she had before when the need to save Jack was urgent and nothing else mattered. She had to keep going and push on to the end. Something was nagging at her though, something that needed addressing before she could pick herself up again.

"Would you do that for me?" Jane asked Ginny, wanting to know if she could trust the girl that until recently had been her adversary. Ginny looked puzzled for a moment but then realised Jane was referring to the sacrifice that David had made to let them get away. She could see Jane was serious and took from her tone that she needed a direct answer, so Ginny stopped trying to move Jane on and thought for a moment.

"The truth is I'm not sure, I've been caught and trapped once already, and I really don't want to be caught again. I felt helpless and suffocated. I couldn't move, I couldn't breathe properly and I thought my eyes were going to pop out I had been upside down for so long. It was terrible, and all the time that I was hanging there I thought the spider was going to come along and suck my insides out while I was still alive. I could smell all the dead people and imagined noises behind me all the time. I don't know if the spider came in or not, I don't know if it thought about eating me. It was awful Jane I really thought I was going to die and I really don't know if I could sacrifice myself like that. If it comes to it, we'll see. We'll see how strong I really am. We'll see if I pass the test. David must really love you though," Ginny concluded, changing the subject.

Jane realised that what Ginny was saying was true and appreciated her honesty. So, David loves me, she thought.

"That complicates things. That means I have to save two

boys." Jane smiled and felt the energy surge back into her. She looked Ginny in the eye. "Okay, I'm ready. I just needed a moment," she explained to Ginny. "And for the record, I don't know if I could do it for you either," she added.

A bang on the door and a heavy scratch that ran the full length of the door stopped their conversation. The door jolted but remained closed, caught on the latch.

"Can we lock it?" Jane asked pushing her weight back against the door and looking for the lock with the head torch in her hand. Jane looked down at the handle; there was a key hole but no key. "There's no key," she added looking around the room for something to prop it closed with. A wooden church pew was on the wall next to the door so Jane ran around the other side of it and pushed it forward across the door.

"The door opens the other way it won't stop it opening," Ginny observed. "Come on let's go before one of its legs catches the door handle," Ginny took control and grabbed Jane as she spoke dragging her towards the stairs and leaving the pew half across the door.

Together they ran the first two flights at speed, grateful for the energy release. The staircase spiralled around the tower and their feet banged out a loud rhythm as they pounded up the stairs. Jane's head torch jumped around erratically as she ran with it in her hand, lighting up the stairs then the ceiling and then the stairs again. Ginny's view from behind was obscured and she just hoped her feet found the next step as she ran. Suddenly Jane stopped. The smell of decay had been getting stronger as she climbed and finally common sense kicked in and she regained control. Ginny stumbled into the back of her but kept her feet.

"Okay we need to calm down," Jane said to herself more than Ginny. "There might be a spider in the tower still, we know there are two. So, we need to go quietly," she said between breaths and forced her breathing to slow down. She could taste the decay as she breathed deeply through her mouth and put her hands to her face to try and block out some of the stench. Behind her Ginny did the same and then spoke in a whisper to Jane above her on the stairs.

"Turn the torch off," she said. Jane turned it off and they were plunged into darkness. Then careful not to drop it she put the torch back into her pocket and gripped the hockey stick with both hands. It was pitch black in the tower stairwell. Jane could not discern any light at all so she leant against the outside wall to keep her balance and slowly started to climb, keeping the hockey stick across her body in front of herself as protection.

Slowly, step by step she moved up in the darkness, the only sounds were the faint sliding of her coat against the wall and her own heartbeat in her ears. Behind her Ginny made no sound at all. Jane had not been in the tower before and did not know how many stairs there were to get to the top or if there was a banister on the inside all the way up. She could sense the drop in the centre of the tower though, through which the bell pulls ran all the way to the church bells at the top, and pushed her shoulder harder against the outside wall to be as far away from the drop as possible.

Jane wanted to breathe deeply to regain her breath and calm her nerves but the air was thick and warm with putrid decay. She took one step at a time and paused on each to listen for any sound, reaching carefully in front of her for any web waiting silently to ensnare her. She was sorely tempted to turn the light on to check if there was a spider in front of her but knew that Ginny was right behind her and would instantly scold her weakness with sharp words. So resolutely she continued up step by step.

She thought back to the cupboard she had shared with Jack earlier. It had seemed pitch black to her in there once the sun had set, but here in the tower the darkness was impenetrable as if it had substance and body. She started to feel dizzy, the steps were uneven and with no visual reference to steady herself she was totally reliant on the outer wall on which she leant heavily for balance. And with every step that she took upwards, the drop down the centre of the tower, just a careless slip away, lengthened.

Jane imagined the injury that she was likely to sustain if she fell from the height she was at as she climbed each step.

"A broken ankle from here," she said to herself as she stepped up and stopped to feel in front of her. "A broken leg now," she said as she took another step. "One broken leg and one broken ankle," she felt around again. "Two broken legs," she muttered to herself.

"Stop it," Ginny interrupted Jane and jabbed her in the back. "I can hear you," she hissed from behind.

Jane sucked in a deep breath of the thick air, it felt like she was sucking the inky blackness in. She wondered if she could catch a disease from the air. It stank so much it must be laden with airborne bits of people, rotted and floating around like dust. She gagged and clenched her eyes and then opened them again as she continued up the stairs following her routine of step and check, step and check. Was there a slight difference in the darkness now? She thought staring into the dark and took another step.

A sound up ahead made her stop. It was a faint rustle and lasted just for a moment. Then Jane heard it again, a slight scratch and she pictured an armoured, black, barbed leg scratching across the floor above. It was the spider. She was certain of it. She clung to the outer wall and looked back.

"I think the spider is just in front of us," she whispered over her shoulder to Ginny.

"Just wait and listen," Ginny urged Jane in reply, aware that Jane was on the verge of turning around.

Jane had steadily slowed as they had climbed and Ginny knew it was nothing to do with tiredness. Jane was a fit, strong girl and the only thing slowing her down was her imagination. Ginny didn't suffer from the fervent imagination that Jane had. She was much more calculating and believed what she could see, not what she could imagine, and right now she could see absolutely nothing. Then she heard it too, it was unmistakeable, three or four scratches just up above, moving away but unmistakeably the sound of a spider scraping and scratching as it walked across the floor above them. Jane turned and pushed against Ginny to get down.

"No," said Ginny and pushed her firmly back up the stairs. "This is the only way we have, we've got to keep going up," she held her ground and took a step up, pushing Jane on. Ginny could feel the hockey stick in Jane's hands resisting her, so she reached up with her free hand to hold it as well.

They both froze, locked together, the scratching from above came again but this time moving towards them.

"It heard you," Ginny accused but was interrupted by the sound of a heavy wooden pew screeching in protest at being pushed over a stone floor and then tipping and crashing down. Ginny turned to face down the stairs and fired the extinguisher to keep the spider back. The extinguisher hissed as it expelled a cloud of gas that filled the stairwell then it stuttered and stopped as the gas ran out. Ginny threw the empty fire extinguisher defiantly down the stairs as she was enveloped in the cold gas cloud. The extinguisher clanked and banged metallically down the stairs taking an age to reach the bottom. The sound echoed and reverberated loudly in the confines of the tower and announced their presence with some certainty, to whatever else was in there with them.

Ginny turned back up the stairs and felt for Jane but she was gone, so on her hands and feet, and holding her breath, she scrambled up the stairs. As she climbed, the darkness gave way, by the time she arrived at the top of the stairs on a wide, open platform the darkness had turned to a murky grey. Ginny could see the church bells mounted on a wooden frame in the centre of the platform. Underneath the bells were the bell rope pulls and the void into which they dangled.

Web crisscrossed the room and cocoons dangled from the high ceiling far out of reach. Dim light came in through openings in the tower walls, openings that had been designed to allow the church bells to toll across the town but now allowed the spider unhindered access to and from the tower. She could see Jane's dark shadow in front of her so she slowly sidled up and whispered in Jane's ear.

"Where is it?" she asked. Jane turned to her and put her mouth to Ginny's ear.

"I can't see it," she replied. "I'm going to turn the torch on, get ready," Jane whispered.

Ginny wasn't quite sure what she was to get ready for, she didn't have the extinguisher anymore and couldn't do much but run. But she clenched her fists and crouched slightly ready for whatever the light revealed.

Jane put the head torch on her head and turned it on. She faced the direction from which she thought the sound had come from and the light immediately illuminated one of the giant spiders, half in and half out of an opening in the far wall. It had a cocooned body in its front legs and was pulling it out after it. The cocoon wriggled in the light and Jane recognised Jack's green duffel coat.

"Jack," she shouted but it was too late, the spider pulled Jack through and disappeared. "I'll find you," she shouted after him. Jane was tempted to run after him but the room was crisscrossed with web.

"Look up," urged Ginny from behind. Jane looked up at the cocoons hanging from the ceiling. There were lots of very small ones. Jane could see a wing and surmised they were mostly birds, pigeons probably, perhaps trying to roost in the tower. But there were three larger ones in the far corner.

Jane shone the torch at them. The first was skeletal and

long dead. It was human but had been consumed and left hanging testament to the spider's thirst for flesh. The second looked straight at Jane. The eyes blinked in the light and then looked away blinded by the bright torch light.

"Mum," shouted Ginny and started to work her way through the gaps in the web to the corner of the room in which her mother was hanging helplessly.

A sound from behind Jane caused her to turn. A black armoured leg covered in sharp bristles was just appearing in the stairwell so without waiting for more of the spider to appear Jane chased after Ginny following her route through the tangled web. She found her in the corner trying to stretch up to reach her mother but to no avail. The spider had suspended her far too high. Ginny's mother had seen the other spider and was shaking her head, frantically declining Ginny's help. She nodded to the opening in the tower wall and screamed from behind the web gag across her mouth.

"Go!" she screamed.

Jane caught up with Ginny, and together they looked back at the spider that had entered the room. It was carrying David and instead of chasing after Jane and Ginny it climbed the wall and moved towards the ceiling. There was a clear route across the ceiling to where Ginny's mother was dangling upside down.

"It's going to hang David from the ceiling," Jane guessed.

Ginny knew they had no chance of rescuing her mother. She was hanging much too high and as soon as the spider had suspended David from the ceiling it would be after them. She thought that they had only two choices. Go back down the staircase or go out after Jack. Jane was already looking out through the opening that the spider had used to leave the tower with Jack.

"It's not far to the church roof from here," she said. The other spider had scuttled upside down across the ceiling now and was busy suspending David next to Ginny's mother.

"Go," said Ginny's mother again, she had tears in her eyes and was trying not to look at the spider next to her. It knocked into her as it worked and she span slowly around and swung forwards and backwards like a pendulum. Ginny tore herself away. She had no words to say to her mother but resolved to herself that she would be back to free her. Undoubtedly the spider would follow her and Jane, so if they could lose it somewhere or even trap it then perhaps she could come back later and free her mother and David.

"Come on," Jane shouted back to Ginny. Jane leant out of the opening and looked down. They weren't quite at the top of the tower, but it was still a long drop to ground level, there was a ledge on the outside wall that ran around the tower, just below the opening, they could use it to climb along and jump down to the church roof. From there they could slide down the roof and jump onto one of the church side buildings. The side buildings were extensions added centuries ago as working accommodation. They were flat pitched and only one storey high. From there it would be a short drop to the ground. The snow was disturbed on top of the nearest roof and this must have been the route the spider carrying Jack had taken. Jane was determined not to think too much and climbed out onto the ledge before her imagination got the better of her.

The air outside was cold and beautifully fresh after the musty, rotted, closeness of the tower and Jane breathed it in gratefully. The hockey stick made it awkward for Jane and she was worried she might lose her grip on the icy stone wall so she threw the stick onto the side building roof to where she was heading. It landed flat and with a puff of snow sunk into a drift. Jane sidestepped along the ledge, facing inwards, her back towards the drop, and headed towards the church roof.

Ginny followed her out, anxious to get out of the tower before the spider finished its work and caught hold of her. There was just enough light thrown back from Jane's head torch for Ginny to place her footing so she sidestepped along carefully in slow pursuit of Jane.

Jane reached the corner of the tower and stepped around it. She was now above the point where the tower joined the church. About ten feet below her the church roof abutted the tower wall. The church roof was steep pitched and rose up from where it met the wall, to a point, high over Jane's head, blocking her view of the town and the cottages on Church Road.

She turned and steadied herself with her back against the wall and then leapt outwards towards the bright circle of light that her head torch lit on the roof. She hit the roof hard and immediately started to slip downwards so she rolled onto her back, raised her feet, and braced ready to impact the tower wall. Her speed picked up quickly on the ice and snow and despite scrabbling with her arms trying frantically to slow her descent she hit the tower wall so heavily that her knees smashed into her chest and for the second time that night the wind was knocked out of her.

In pain and gasping for breath Jane pushed up with her legs to take the pressure off her chest and tried to suck air into her empty lungs.

"That went well," remarked Ginny from above peering around the corner. She could see why Jane had jumped, the church roof seemed tantalisingly close however it was so steep and icy that jumping to it only resulted in a sudden plummet to the tower wall. Ginny decided a different approach was necessary, and so, turned and crouched down balancing carefully, then sat down on the ledge with her back against the wall. Then putting her hands to one side on the ledge, she swung down so that she was hanging under the ledge. From there she found a foothold and a handhold and climbed down half a body length before dropping down and landing lightly on her feet next to Jane.

"Ready?" she asked Jane.

Jane nodded still feeling the effects of the fall and pushed herself to her feet.

"You can go off people you know," she replied.

Ginny took the lead now and edged around the tower and looked down. The side building was about six feet down and the same along. Ginny was pretty sure she could make it if she just got enough purchase to push off properly from the tower. She kicked away the snow and ice from her jumping point and then crouched and jumped. The drop to the ground below flashed dizzyingly underneath her and then her feet landed on the flat pitched roof of the side building. Her momentum carried her forward so she rolled in the snow and came to her feet poised ready to run or fight.

Jane's head torch had followed her like a spot light following an actor on a stage then it was Jane's turn. The bright light made it difficult for Ginny to watch Jane so she turned away and started searching for the hockey stick buried under the snow, consequently she didn't see the first of the spider's legs coming out of the tower.

Jane positioned herself exactly as Ginny had done. The drop to the ground was a long way down and quite distracting from the actual jump that she had to make to the roof. She crouched and leant forward over the jump and then inadvertently looked down away from the safety of the side building roof to the drop below, and all strength left her legs. The torchlight reflected off the white snow far below, it glittered like diamonds and looked strangely inviting as if it would cushion and envelop her like when she flopped face down onto her duvet covered bed at home. She was cold and tired, the impact with the tower wall had knocked her confidence, and the jump seemed too far, perhaps if she just let go she could rest in the snow. Jane closed her eyes and hung there by one hand leaning out over the drop.

Unknown to Jane, a wheelbarrow and gardening tools lay under the snow waiting for her. A shovel, a pick and sharp gardening shears all hidden under the thick blanket, hard and unyielding they waited to smash her body. Jane looked up and opened her eyes.

"It can't end like this, I've got to make the jump," she encouraged herself. A flicker of movement caught her eye and she looked to her left just in time to see the spider reaching out towards her. It recoiled in the sudden flash of light from the head torch, and Jane, sensing she would have only one chance, leapt without even looking where she was going to land.

A sudden rush of adrenalin fuelled her leap and she sailed across the gap and crashed onto the flat roof. It was an ungainly landing and her head and outstretched arms plunged under the snow. It filled her mouth and froze her neck and face in a sudden icy rush. She came to her feet spluttering, crawling and scrabbling away from the drop that she was already well clear of, and the spider that she had left on the tower wall.

Ginny had seen the spider now and pulled Jane up by yanking on the hood of her coat. She had reclaimed the hockey stick from the snow that Jane had taken from Ginny's mother's car and now intended to keep hold of it. Jane was still struggling and coughing out chunks of snow as they approached the edge of the roof. Ginny looked back, the spider was scuttling around the tower, and would soon be across the church roof and onto the same roof as them. She hauled Jane forwards and pushed her off as she jumped herself, blindly, down to the ground below.

Jane's head torch lit up a wild arc in the snow as the ground rushed up and they landed on their feet softly in a large drift at the edge of the church graveyard. Ginny pulled Jane from the drift as Jane regained her breath.

"Wait, wait," Jane shouted as Ginny tugged at her. "We're running away from one spider and chasing another, it's insane. We need help we can't do this on our own anymore. We need a plan and we need help." Jane had a hold of the lapels on Ginny's coat and was desperately shouting into Ginny's face. Ginny reached up to the head torch still strapped on Jane's head and turned it off and looked around the graveyard before she answered.

The clouds that had dulled the winter evening earlier had receded, and now the night had set in, the stars and moon provided light by which Ginny could pick out the hunched shoulders of gravestones crouching in the dark. The white snow that still lay heavily on the ground, and had been given an icy crust by the day's sun and the night's chill, marked out the bases of the gravestones and provided a white path through the throng of stone statues. The graveyard was still and quiet and Ginny could not pinpoint any danger but knew that the spider on the roof would catch them up momentarily.

She thought quickly. The church nave seemed like the only viable trap. It had a way in through which they could draw the spiders and a second exit through which she and Jane could escape, they just needed a way of securing the doors.

"We need to double back through the church and trap the spiders there," she told Jane, although she didn't add that she didn't know how to do that yet. Jane thought about Ginny's plan.

"Okay but we need to catch up to the spider with Jack and then get both spiders to chase us to the church. One of us will need to run through and close the tower door and one will need to hide behind the main door and jump out once the spiders are in the church and close the main door," Jane said, neatly finishing off Ginny's plan. A sound above them made them both look up. The spider behind crunched in the icy snow on the roof and dislodged a clump from the edge that dropped to the ground. "I'm not going in the tower again," added Jane as they ran out into the graveyard away from the spider behind them and toward the spider with Jack.

Chapter 20

Jane edged ahead of Ginny as they ran into the graveyard, spurred on partly by her need to find Jack, and partly by an unconscious need to stay ahead of Ginny to avoid being the first of the two of them that the pursuing spider could catch. She ran crouched, treading lightly to try to avoid crunching the icy crust on the snow unnecessarily, and turned her head left and right, looking for danger as they headed deeper into the graveyard.

Ginny settled in behind Jane and tried to step into the footprints that Jane left in the snow and reduce the sound that she made as she ran. She glanced back and saw the spider was just reaching ground level, and to her horror, in her periphery, she saw another creature cutting in from the church and running parallel to Jane and her through the graves.

"Jane, look over to your left!" she jabbered out in warning.

Jane glanced left and saw the creature straight away. It ran quickly until it was level with her and then slowed to keep pace and maintain its distance. It looked to its right, straight at Jane, and Jane thought in the half-light that it was the same creature that she had trapped in the car earlier. It wasn't running easily, its tongue lolled out as if it was exhausted, and it was favouring one of its front legs. It ran through a patch of light, thrown out carelessly by a church window, and Jane saw its teeth and mouth were bloodstained, and it was bleeding heavily from a wound on its leg. It had obviously been in a fight with something and hadn't had it all its own way.

The creature started to curve its run towards Jane, so she curved hers to maintain the gap, and then saw the spider on the other side of her. It scuttled along on the snow on its eight legs, going easily over the top of the gravestones, and only weaving around the largest of statues. As Jane turned towards it; it turned away to keep the distance between them the same. Jane looked back and nearly stumbled. Ginny was right behind, and behind her the spider that had been following them had closed right up and now also appeared to be maintaining its distance. Jane stretched out her legs and increased her speed and all the creatures speeded up with her. Then she slowed down and they all slowed as well. The fox creature closed in suddenly again and snarled viciously at Jane. She turned away and again the spider on her right veered away to maintain the gap.

"They're herding us," she told Ginny, grabbing her by the arm and slowing down to a walk. All the creatures slowed as well, the spiders were silent except for their feet crunching in the snow and scratching on the stone gravestones, and the fox creature snarled loudly and growled deep in its chest. The odd formation ground to a halt and eyed each other suspiciously.

"They're herding us," Jane said again, as she realised that she was correct. The spider behind took a step towards them and they took a step away. It took another step forward and together Ginny and Jane moved away and started to walk slowly in the direction they were being herded. The creature's efforts were coordinated and they worked as a team to move Jane and Ginny forward. The girls were holding onto each other and looking around hurriedly.

Ginny hadn't seen the fox creature until now and she was horrified by it. She had been caught by a spider and escaped relatively unscathed, but the creature on her left was something else entirely. It appeared and disappeared as it passed behind the gravestones and statues, sometimes in shadow and sometimes dimly visible. The occasional light from the church picked out the powerful muscles in its hunched shoulders, its face was dog-like but flattened and its blood-stained teeth were bared aggressively. Ginny had no idea what to do if it attacked but knew that if it did, she would have no chance of walking away unscathed. It growled under her stare, a growl so deep it seemed to Ginny that she felt, rather than heard it. The growl rattled around inside the creature, restrained by its deep chest and laden with pent up violence. It was unable to bear its weight on one of its front legs, but this just seemed to make it angrier, Ginny decided her only hope would be to outrun the lame creature and vowed not to face it no matter what happened.

She had an irrational thought that seduced her mind and taunted her that perhaps she had been better off when she was trapped in the web. It had been simple then and maybe she would have been rescued when this was all over, she didn't want to be the one that had to risk her life running around a graveyard. Perhaps this was Jane's fault! The thought buzzed around in her head like an annoying fly that she was unable to swat. Jane pulled at her arm to attract her attention and the elusive thought disappeared.

"Look," Jane said pointing to their front in the direction in which they were being herded.

A red glow was visible up ahead in the darkness. It pulsated and seemed to increase and decrease in strength. Jane knew instantly what it was.

"It's coming from the statue of Alfred," she told Ginny. "I went there earlier and the statue came to life. Alfred's trapped in it, and his brother, the one that lives at the cottage with the spider. He's going to bring him back to life. Oh, wait you know that bit, you were listening when we were in the web. Okay the statue is the key to it all and that's where Alfred is, and he is using this lot to herd us to him." Jane pointed at the spiders and towards the red glow as if she was directing traffic, her words spilled out to their inevitable conclusion.

"We might not be in cocoons Ginny, but we're as trapped as the rest of them. What are we going to do?" she asked in a high-pitched voice that revealed the fear within her.

Ginny looked around again. They were nearing the red glow now and the creatures around them continued to keep pace.

"We wait Jane," Ginny told her. "And when the moment is right we run, we run as fast as we can and we don't look back and we don't stop. We run to my house and we lock ourselves in and call the police. This is too big for us Jane; we can't hope to win." Ginny spoke calmly but rapidly in hushed tones to not alert anyone of their plan. And while she was talking she resolved to run and keep running even if Jane wasn't with her. The only way she could help Jane now was to alert the police and get them to come to her aid.

"We have to wait until the moment is right though," Ginny took hold of Jane's shoulders and pressed her fingers down hard. "You have to wait Jane, wait for the right moment. I'll tell you when to run," she instructed.

Jane gulped and nodded, she would trust her friend and wait until their moment to run presented itself, and then as soon as Ginny told her to, she would run as hard as she could. Jane looked at Ginny and believed that Ginny would help her when the moment was right.

The glow was close now, the girls rounded a tall stone cross, mounted on a plinth that had been obscuring their view, and entered the small clearing around Alfred's statue. Their arrival was met with hysterical laughter and they saw Alfred Thatcher on the other side of the clearing, laughing and clapping his hands in sarcastic welcome. His grin was maniacal and his eyes were wide open and staring.

"You were right Alfred, you were right," he laughed to the statue of his older brother. "Here they are, like lambs to the slaughter, just as you said they would be," he said, almost patting the statue of Alfred on the back in congratulation but withdrawing his hand quickly before it was burnt by the heat within the stone.

Alfred, the shame of Middle Gratestone, leant out of his statue and twisted to look at the girls. His bright red ethereal form hung down as if manacled at the wrist by the stone. His hands twisted and turned in a constant battle to free themselves, his body was tense and his face creased with the effort of pulling himself from the statue.

His red ghostly form was dressed in the rags in which he had fallen on the day he died and his eyes burned like fire. He sneered in contempt, as he saw the girls, and the rage that burned within him turned the clearing red. The snow had melted in a circle around him and the ground was softened and yielding underfoot.

At the base of the stone plinth, on which his statue was mounted, lay a cocooned body unmoving on the ground, a green duffel coat hood was clearly visible at one end. The girls felt the heat from where they stood, it warmed their faces in dangerous wafts, like an out of control fire, hot and mesmerising but too dangerous to approach.

Alfred smiled humourlessly at them, sensing victory was at hand. Sensing that his time to return to the land of the living had arrived with the arrival of the girls, and that the century he had spent trapped in a statue watching the townsfolk pass by was finally over.

Time had not mellowed Alfred, he had been deeply wronged and every child that hurried by the church graveyard, too afraid to look at him, reminded him of his childhood innocence that had been so cruelly stolen. He had watched children grow old as he should have grown old, and then he had watched their children grow old. And all the time he had felt like he was being mocked.

'Look at what you could have had. You could have had a childhood. You could have had a life. You could have run and laughed and loved and lived. But you can't because they killed you. They killed your parents, they killed your brother, they took your home and your money, and they took your life.'

"Argh!" screamed Alfred. He pulsed brighter as he screamed out his hatred at the girls. Here they were at last the descendants of the baker that had starved him, and the mayor that had been the ringleader of the cartel that had robbed him of his home, money and life. And before him on the ground the descendant of the boy that had delivered the final blow and sent his cold hungry body crashing to the snow-covered ground one hundred years ago.

"Argh!" he screamed again, and flashed red, sparks shot out from his mouth like spit, and flames dripped from his hands and fizzed out on the ground. Beside him Alfred Thatcher laughed high pitched hysterical laughter, clapped his hands, and jumped up and down like a child receiving a new toy as a present, adding his laughter to the cacophony.

"Argh!" Alfred screamed at them again, his form burst briefly into flames and then returned to red. Alfred Thatcher laughed and continued to clap at his brother's display of power and fury.

Jane could stand by no longer, she had been trying to find Jack all night, and so, now that she could finally reach him, she rushed into the clearing against the heat emanating from Alfred and grabbed Jack's hood with both hands and started to pull him across the ground back towards Ginny. Jack was heavy and her progress was slow, one heave at a time. She strained and struggled as she dragged him, her feet slipped on the snow melt as she fought to keep momentum.

Ginny walked over once Jane was halfway back and stood guard with the hockey stick as Jane continued to grunt and strain as she pulled Jack along, until they were back to where the girls had entered the clearing. A spider prevented any further progress out of the clearing, and so Jane set about freeing Jack from the sticky web that bound him. She ripped the strands from his face and pulled back the hood of Jack's coat, he took a deep breath and smiled up at her, then just as quickly the smile was gone and a shadow passed across his face.

"I'm glad to see you, but you shouldn't be here Jane. They mean to kill us," he told her. There was desperation in his voice and in his eyes. Jane could see that the time he had spent in the spider's web had sapped his strength and he had all but given up and accepted his fate. But as he looked at Jane the love welled up inside him and provided him with the motivation he needed, he refuted that her fate was to die in this graveyard tonight, and started to struggle out of the web.

Jane watched the fight come back into his eyes, the Jack that Jane knew, returned and his mouth set into a determined line. She continued to pull the web away from him and once his hands were free Jack helped and then together they stood and hugged one another.

"Are you alright?" he asked softly brushing at a hair on her forehead.

"I'm fine Jack," Jane replied.

"We've been trying to find you," she said looking at Ginny and waving an arm in her direction.

"Hello Ginny," greeted Jack, seemingly noticing Ginny for the first time.

"Jack," said Ginny curtly, holding her hockey stick across herself, both in defence against the creatures around her, and against the display of affection next to her.

Ginny had always known that Jack preferred Jane and had always known that one day they would end up together. It upset her the way that Jack and Jane always looked at each other and upset her even more that even though Jane had clearly won Jack's affection she still found the need to be disparaging and mean to Ginny. Jane had eroded their friendship and left Ginny without a boyfriend and a best friend. Looking at them together now Ginny felt a flare of jealousy and the comradeship she and Jane had recently shared seemed pointless and diminished. Perhaps she should just run now and leave them to it, she thought.

"Death!" screamed Alfred interrupting Ginny's thoughts. The voice of Alfred seemed to come from all around them. It had no central source and filled the clearing with noise. Alfred's mouth clearly moved as he spoke but the sound didn't emanate from him.

"Death!" he screamed again, the sound once again coming from everywhere. Ginny checked behind her to see if there was another Alfred there but only the spider met her gaze with its black unblinking eyes.

"Death, come to me," Alfred called out. His voice was still loud but much more measured. "Come and accept my exchange," he shouted.

"Yes, yes," clapped Alfred Thatcher still bouncing up and down.

Ginny had listened to Alfred Thatcher's story that he had told Jane in the kitchen earlier. There were elements of it that she still found hard to believe but as Alfred called for Death she found herself looking around nervously for someone or something to appear. She searched the darkness between the statues and gravestones dotted around the graveyard outside the circle of red light looking to see something but hoping that she wouldn't see anything. And then she saw it. Or, rather she didn't.

A dark shadow moved through the graveyard towards the clearing. It was like a dark mist, an absence of light that moved steadily, passing through and over gravestones and statues, rather than around them. It left them darkened and spoiled in its wake, lichen and moss that had been clinging to life on the hard stone, blackened and died as the shadow passed, and as it reached the clearing the grass underfoot withered in silent agony.

Ginny recognised Death from her dreams. She had long suffered a repeating dream of being chased by this dark mass through streets and across fields. She had always awoken from her dream in terror, with her sweat soaked bed sheets sticking to her, before the darkness had caught her, but she knew that if it ever did that she would surely die. Her knees trembled and her legs threatened to run her away from the clearing of their own volition. She was scared now, more scared than she had ever been before.

Jane too saw Death. But she saw it differently to Ginny. She saw Death as a white angel, seemingly carved from stone, as had been described to her by her grandmother when Granddad had died.

'A beautiful white angel with wings and a halo, has taken him away to heaven,' her grandmother had told her. 'There he will live in the clouds with his friends and family, having fun, singing songs and even playing tricks on people like he used to do to you as you were growing up.'

The angel glided across the graveyard in the air, beautiful and serene. But as it approached and came into full view in the harsh red light, Jane's fear disfigured it. The angel of Death had no eyes and her teeth were uncovered in her lipless mouth, the teeth were blackened, sharpened to points and dangerous. The hands just visible under a white shawl that hung from her shoulders were three fingered and vulture-like, clawed and scaled they were useless for anything except stripping flesh from bone. A scythe like sword hung from her waist, and battle-scarred armour covered her breast. Jane gripped Jack by the arm and stared at the angel of Death before her.

Alfred Thatcher, surprised by the appearance of Death next to him cowered and held his hands over his head in defence. He whimpered and moved close to the statue of his brother where emboldened again he clapped and laughed nervously and waited for his brother to speak.

"Fulfil your promise to my father and bring me back to life," Alfred said in a clear voice unburdened by fear but tarnished with petulant impatience.

"All is to remain in balance, for one to live one must die," a voice said in Jane's head. It was her voice, her own private voice. The one that spoke in her head when she was thinking or reading to herself, it didn't have sound but it was hers nonetheless and it spoke to her now.

"A choice must be made," the voice in Jane's head said. "It must be made by one of you." Jane looked at her vision of Death, and realised she was being given a choice. Then in horror she realised that she was being given a choice about who should die to enable Alfred to live.

Jane looked at Jack. He looked as appalled as Jane felt and looked Jane in the eye. Jane realised that they had all been given the same choice.

"Nobody choose!" she instructed her friends quickly. "Think about something else, just don't make a choice." she shook Jack's arm as she spoke. "Think of something else," she urged.

"I'm trying to," replied Jack. "I don't want to choose, okay football teams in the premiership. Manchester United, Chelsea, Liverpool, Arsenal," Jack started to reel off football teams, quickly at first and then a little slower so as not to run out of teams too quickly. Alfred Thatcher's laughter cut across them.

"Choose, choose," he laughed. The red ethereal ghost of Alfred leant out of the statue and watched them intently and then smiled malevolently as Death moved past him towards the group of terrified teenagers.

Jane's inner voice spoke in her head again. They weren't her words but they were in her voice and they punched through her thoughts, violating her mind.

"A choice has been made," Death said simply, and silence descended on the clearing. The two Alfreds looked on expectantly and Jane and Jack looked around in surprise. Ginny was the first to break the silence as Death glided up to the group and stopped in front of them.

"I'm sorry Jane," Ginny apologised. Jane and Jack looked at her, mortified.

"What have you done?" asked Jack urgently in a quiet voice that carried weight despite its lack of volume.

"I made a choice," said Ginny. "Someone had to, so I did. I made a choice." She sounded certain of herself.

Jane looked hard at Ginny. Ginny looked sad but calm, lucid and determined. Her face distorted and swam in Jane's vision as tears filled Jane's eyes, the memories of how she had treated Ginny over recent years all rushed back to her. She had ignored Ginny. She had spoken about Ginny behind her back, sniping at her to anyone that would listen. She had deliberately not passed on messages from teachers so that Ginny would get in trouble and at every opportunity she had tried to separate Ginny from Jack.

She hadn't spoken a polite word to her for over two years and always fired dark nasty looks at her back in full view of all their schoolmates. Jane knew she had conducted a nasty, illicit, childish campaign against Ginny. She knew it was wrong and wished she could take it back. They had bonded again tonight and Jane had hoped now that they could be friends but it had been too little too late and now it was time for Ginny to get payback.

"What have you done to me?" asked Jane already knowing the answer.

Death reached out an upturned hand. Jane looked down at the vulture's claw extended in front of her, it closed under her gaze into a fist, and Jane closed her eyes and waited for her heart to be crushed into useless pulp. A second passed, she could feel her pulse beating ferociously in her neck and her breathing shortened and she tensed her muscles hard. She knew this was the end. Ginny had made a choice and had chosen her. Jack might mourn her for a while but in the end, he would move on and Ginny would get her man. Jane felt no anger towards Ginny, she knew she deserved it and for a fleeting moment just wished that she had behaved better toward her, perhaps then things would be different now.

The sound of a body falling hard on the ground caused Jane to open her eyes again. The white angel that was her vision of Death still stood in front of them and for a moment Jane thought that she must be dead. But when she looked around she saw that it was Ginny lying lifeless on the floor. Her legs were folded under her as if she had just dropped where she stood, and her arms were spread wide. She looked peaceful but her beautiful clear skin was porcelain white and her lips blue. The only colour on her cheeks was from the red glow of Alfred, who still burned intensely hanging from his statue.

Jane's white angel of Death turned. A long white robe hung down between the folded wings on her back and masked her feet. She glided, just off the ground, away from Jane and Jack and left them alone with Ginny's lifeless body.

"No," said Jane so quietly as to be barely audible. She was mortified at Ginny's death. Amazed by Ginny's bravery, and saddened by her own weakness. Even as Ginny had chosen herself, so that Jack and Jane could live, Jane had thought the worst of her. She had believed that Ginny had chosen Jane to die so that she might have Jack to herself, when Ginny had selflessly volunteered for death in order to save her friends.

Jane cried out and fell to her knees. She was disgusted with herself, and abhorred by her lack of strength and trust, and totally desolate by the loss of Ginny.

The two brothers laughed as Death passed in front of them, although Alfred Thatcher pulled back nervously as Death moved by, but once Death had moved to the edge of the clearing Alfred Thatcher stepped out confidently, laughing loudly and pointing at Ginny's lifeless body.

"She chose herself," he laughed in disbelief. "And you thought she had chosen you," he pointed accusingly at Jane. "What have you done to me?" he mocked Jane in a high-pitched imitation of her voice, and then laughed at his impression. "I bet you wouldn't have chosen yourself, would you? No, you're the scared one. I bet you would have seen all your friends die in front of you before you chose yourself. You would have chosen them one after the other. It's written all over your face. Fear, disgust, self-loathing, it's all there." Alfred Thatcher mocked Jane as he walked towards her, away from the relative safety next to his brother and out into the open clearing.

Jane looked up from the floor. She didn't care what happened to her now. She didn't care if she lived or died. Anger at the man in front of her slowly took hold and replaced the fear that had eaten away at her like a cancer, consuming flesh. The hockey stick lay on the ground next to Ginny's body. Jane took a hold of it, stood up, and looked at Alfred Thatcher with murder in her eyes.

"You won't live to see your brother returned," she spat at Alfred Thatcher.

"Don't hurt me," Alfred raised his hands in mock surrender and took a step back, clearly not worried at all by Jane's threat. Jack moved to Jane's shoulder and clenched his fists.

"For Ginny," he said.

"For Ginny," Jane repeated through clenched teeth and took a step towards Alfred Thatcher.

A vicious growl stopped her, and the fox creature limped into the clearing. Although injured, it was still formidable, and Jane and Jack were no match for it. Snarling, frothing blood, and snapping its teeth, it moved to block Jane and Jack's advance.

"Thank you, brother," said Alfred to his brother who was still restrained by the statue but was obviously the puppet master controlling the strings of the spiders and the vicious fox creature. Death had gone beyond the boundary of the clearing now and was making its way out of the circle of light.

Jane gripped her hockey stick tightly as the fox creature hunched its powerful shoulders and prepared to pounce, when suddenly and unexpectedly, a stream of liquid jetted out of the darkness and hit the creature in the face. It jumped back in surprise and then yelped in pain and danced around shaking its head and screwing its eyes up tight.

A second stream of liquid came from the shadows and hit a surprised Alfred Thatcher. He shouted out in alarm and then in pain.

"It's burning me," he shouted. An acrid burning smell spread around the clearing and Jane covered her mouth and nose to prevent herself from being affected. Alfred Thatcher clawed at his face and eyes, and the fox creature ran howling out of the clearing.

Jane looked into the darkness to try to find the source of the stream of liquid, and saw a dark figure emerge from the gloom into the red light of the clearing.

"Dad!" shouted Jack in recognition as Henry Rogers came into view.

Henry was in bad shape, his sleeves were in rags and his arms and hands were dripping blood. One trouser leg was ripped open and a deep gash was visible through the tear. He was ashen white and limping terribly, but he didn't hesitate for one second, and punched Alfred Thatcher as hard as he could straight between Alfred's raised hands. Alfred's eyes were closed and the attack was both ferocious and devastating. Alfred's nose smashed in a spray of blood. Shock numbed the pain, and unconsciousness tried to shut down his mind, and hide the truth of this unkind turn of events. His knees buckled and he staggered backwards, arms flailing, until his balance deserted him and he fell out of control, totally unaware of his surroundings. He fell as if he expected to land on a feather bed, or a crowd of outstretched arms reaching out to break his fall and lower him gently to the ground, but reality was not so kind.

The back of his head smashed onto solid marble, bone cracked and splintered and his brain stem was crushed and rendered into useless unconnected tissue, nerve and bone. Unconsciousness had already taken him and now life instantly left him for Death to claim. His body was beyond repair and at the edge of light and darkness, just before departing from sight, Death stopped and looked back towards the clearing.

Henry Rogers gathered Jack and Jane to him. Jack

hugged him in relief and then pulled away, his hands wet and sticky with his father's blood.

"Dad what happened to you?" he asked taking some of his father's weight on his shoulder.

"Dog trouble," Henry replied. "But at least it led me here," he added with a strained half smile and ruffled his son's hair with a bloodied hand.

Alfred looked from left to right, he didn't seem concerned by his brother's demise, and he looked from his brother's body, to Ginny's body, to the throng hugging in front of him, and to Death, slowly approaching the clearing. Death spoke to them.

"All must return to balance," the voice in Jane's head informed her. Jane looked around unsure what this meant. Death stood by Alfred Thatcher's body for a moment, waved a hand, and then glided away back into the darkness. Just for a second Jane thought she saw someone following Death, but when she looked again there was nobody there.

To Jane's right Ginny gasped and sucked in a lung full of air. She breathed in long and deep as if she had just returned to air after a long dive underwater.

"Ginny!" exclaimed Jane and rushed to help her friend. She helped Ginny to sit and then hugged her tightly.

"I'm so sorry," she apologised, knowing now that Ginny had never deserted her as a friend. Ginny pulled back and looked at Jane.

"I passed the test," she said.

"Yes!" replied Jane. "You got one hundred percent, top marks. Yes, you passed the test. Are you okay?" Jane asked, concerned and desperately worried that Ginny would be taken away again. She looked around for danger.

The spiders still lurked at the fringes but for now appeared content just to prevent their departure. The fox creature howled and yapped in the distance and Alfred remained tethered by his wrists to the statue. Death reached the edge of the red glow that shone from Alfred, and disappeared into the darkness.

Alfred watched Death, until he could see it no more and then looked at Jane. Their eyes met for a moment, then peace seemed to come over Alfred, he closed his eyes and relaxed into the statue of himself, and then unexpectedly, burst into intense flame. It was sudden and so bright that the flash burned Jane's eyes, as if she had glanced at the sun. She snapped her gaze away and shielded her eyes. Jack and his father were still in the centre of the clearing and they staggered back away from the inferno and hurried over to Jane and Ginny. They all crouched and looked away from the intense light. Wind whipped up around them and brought in blasts of cold air that alternated with waves of heat from Alfred.

Jane tucked her head down, shielded her face and screamed into the wind. Her scream was whipped away and she heard echoes of voices as the wind tore around them.

"All must return to balance."

"For Ginny."

"Death, come to me..." and other unintelligible garbling as time rewound.

Alfred Thatcher's hysterical laughter echoed through it all. Then just as suddenly as it had started, it stopped with a loud resonating crack and the sound of something falling to the ground.

Calm and darkness descended on the clearing and the small group remained quiet and motionless in a huddle crouched on the ground. Jane had her eyes tight shut but when she felt the wind drop and the heat disappear from the side of her face, she opened them and looked around. She still had a flaming red image of Alfred on fire, blinding her vision, and it moved wherever she looked. The clearing was dark and Jane could not see past the image and into the darkness to see the statue of Alfred or the red ghostly Alfred that had been trapped within it.

Henry Rogers was the first to act. He took his torch from its holster on his belt and turned it on. First, he flashed it around their little gang crouched on the floor.

"Is everyone okay?" he asked. Jack, Ginny and Jane all replied at once speaking over each other and then Jane followed Henry's lead and turned her head torch on as Henry swung his torch around to light up the statue of Alfred.

The statue was cracked clean into two pieces, it was split down the middle, and one half lay toppled on the ground, while the other remained upright but was leant over in the other direction. At the base of the stone plinth on which the statue had been mounted was a small figure on hands and knees, dressed in tough leather boots, faded blue trousers tied at the waist with a rope, and a threadbare cotton shirt patched at the elbows. His head was in his hands, and as they watched, he slowly sat up onto his knees and blinked through his fingers in the light from the two torches.

Henry and Jane instinctively pointed their torches

slightly away so as not to blind the new arrival and in return he uncovered his face and looked back at the people behind the torchlight. Jane and Ginny gasped in amazement together. The likeness of the boy before them to the statue now split in two was staggering. He had strong cheekbones and even at his young age was handsome.

"Alfred," said Jane first, coming to the same conclusion as all the others. The boy shivered as the heat that had burned so intensely a moment ago dissipated and was replaced by the bitter chill of winter.

"Where am I?" Alfred asked in a young clear voice. There was no hint of malevolence or anger, and the intensity of his glare and the furrows in his brow had lessened. He had lost the red glow and he had a sense of nervousness and temerity about him, like a kitten venturing outside for the first time. He spoke again in a voice that was centred at its source and drew their eyes to him rather than cause them to look around for a second speaker. He was flesh and blood and as he knelt and took in his surroundings he simply seemed to be a lost confused young boy. He was breathing quickly and his breath clouded the air around him and created shadows on the gravestones behind. "I was next to the church," he said and touched his nose gingerly in unsure memory and looked around as if trying to connect what he could recall with what he could see now.

Jane recalled that Alfred had died next to the church and felt a rush of sympathy for him and started to feel protective of him. She suddenly remembered that Alfred had a brother, and she looked for Alfred Thatcher's body, in the hope that she could hide it, and in doing so prevent Alfred from suffering the sight of it, albeit that Alfred would probably not recognise the grown man that Alfred Thatcher had become.

Jane stood up and tried to look for the body without shining the head torch directly at it and alerting Alfred to its presence, but she was unable to find it. Curious she moved closer to where Alfred Thatcher had fallen and used the head torch to light up the ground. The grass was dried and singed all around the clearing except for a man-sized area where Alfred Thatcher's body had been. But other than the imprint of his large frame there was no sign of him. Jane was certain that he was dead, not just because of the sickening noise that his head had made when it hit the stone plinth, but also because Death had appeared to claim him and returned Ginny to them. She looked around and then turned to the boy on the ground as everyone else slowly got to their feet and gathered around.

"I'm Jane," she said and stuck out a hand. "Can I help you up?" she asked, certain now that the boy before her was not a threat. The boy hesitated for a second and then in a leap of faith took Jane's proffered hand. She pulled him to his feet and they stood toe to toe.

Although Jane was older they were similar in height and looked directly at each other while their right hands remained in a tight embrace.

"My name is Alfred," said Alfred in response to Jane's introduction. "You said my name just then but I don't know you," he stated, his hand was cool in Jane's grasp and she was certain now that Alfred's quest to be restored to life had worked, but that this was not the Alfred that had been trapped inside the statue for one hundred years, this was Alfred the boy, who had died in the graveyard one hundred years ago. He was not embittered by a century of hate and was here because of an act of kindness by his own father as he died on the battlefield, and the result of Death fulfilling the promise made to Alfred's father.

The sound of distant police sirens penetrated the night and the cluster of people in the graveyard looked around.

"I called it in before I used the pepper spray," Henry Rogers explained. "In a minute or two this place will be full of police, everyone's coming," he walked around the clearing using his flash light to search the surrounding area. The beam of light picked out crosses, angels and gravestones one after the other like a flickering black and white movie jumping from frame to frame and then it picked out one of the spiders. It was motionless, but as soon as the torchlight fell on it, it burst into life and tried to sidestep out of the light. It staggered as it did so and with a wet crunching crack one of its legs stuck in the snow and detached from its socket in the creature's abdomen. Thick green liquid spurted out from the socket in two separate distinct spurts and then dribbled to the floor. The spider staggered, leaving its detached leg standing upright in the snow and tripped over a gravestone. The armoured carapace over its head cracked open and more green fluid oozed out. Lumps and bumps bubbled up on its distended abdomen and stretched the skin tight and then shrank back to normal as if something inside the creature was moving around and trying to escape. A huge lump appeared on top of its abdomen and the spider's skin stretched taut and thinned to breaking point.

"It's going to explode," said Jack. And as if prophesised, the lump burst and a fountain of green bodily liquid sprayed into the air as a pink human arm punched through the skin and reached out to the sky. The fingers extended and clawed at the night air as if searching for something to grip on to, and haul the rest of the pink body out from the spider into the open. Then the spider succumbed to the parasitic attack, fell backwards, and with a gurgle, disappeared.

"Alright," said Henry Rogers taking charge, and completely ignoring the exploding spider as if it had never happened. Loss of blood and the onset of shock dulled his curiosity and he stoically and protectively moved to get the children out of harm's way. "Let's get out of the graveyard and back to the road. There's a lot more police coming and right now we need to keep you lot safe until they get here." Procedure drove Henry now, and as he fought against his injuries and exhaustion, he hung onto the police procedures that had been ingrained into him.

"What's that noise?" asked Alfred clearly unfamiliar with the sound of police sirens.

"I need to find my mum, she's still in the church tower," said Ginny blocking Henry's path out of the graveyard.

"Look," said Henry. I don't understand what has happened here tonight but it's late. You kids need to get home to your parents and into bed. The police can sort out this mess–and what happened–and who was involved tomorrow. Ginny you're going to hospital, something strange happened to you tonight," Henry told her.

"I need to get my mum!" Ginny protested.

"The police will handle that, I'll get people up in the tower straight away," Henry placated Ginny. "This is police business now and this is a crime scene. We need to get you all out of here right now. Okay that's it, move to the road," Henry ordered and ushered everyone gently towards Church Road.

The sirens were loud now and the group headed out of the clearing. Alfred was the last to leave. Henry placed a hand around his shoulder, but before Alfred left the clearing he looked back at the split statue for a moment and smiled an unseen smile, and then turned and followed the others.

The girls hung on to each other, and cast continuous curious glances in Alfred's direction. They wanted to help him, but even though they were convinced he was just a boy, they could not easily forget the events of that night. Jack hovered anxiously around his bleeding father, and Alfred remained apart as he had been in his statue trapped in the graveyard for one hundred years. He shivered in the cold, as the flashing lights approached, and waited for the rest of his life to start.

Chapter 21

After tossing and turning in bed for what seemed a very short time, the following morning started relatively normally for Jane. She was woken early by her mother who explained that the police wanted them to report to school together that morning at the usual time. Breakfast was already on the table in the kitchen when Jane arrived downstairs in fresh uniform. She was unable to eat much though, and nibbled on some toast that she washed down, one mouthful at a time, with cold orange juice. Her mother walked with Jane to school, and for the first time in three years, Jane allowed her to do so without complaint. The paths on either side of Church Road were closed and Jane and her mother had to be cleared through a police cordon to pass the church.

Various white police tents of different shapes and sizes had been erected and were dotted about in the graveyard, faceless people dressed in white hooded overalls and masks were busying themselves around the site, and hurried in and out of the tents. The snow had been trampled down by the multitude of feet and lay about like clods of grey dirt. Jane and her mother were escorted through by a uniformed police officer and hurried away as quickly as they could. It was unusual for Jane to complete this part of the walk to school with so many other people present, however she passed through, for the first time ever, without experiencing the feeling of being watched.

Jack was waiting for Jane at the crossroads. He was also with his mother, and Jane and Jack hugged each other while the two parents started to animatedly discuss what each of them knew about the previous night's events.

"Are you okay?" Jack asked. He sounded a little nervous and Jane surmised that like her, he was worried that everything would be different now. That they had all changed in some way. She was comforted by his concern though.

"I'm tired but good," she reassured him. "How is your dad?" she asked touching Jack gently on the arm.

"He's okay," Jack replied. "He's been released from hospital. They had to put over fifty stitches in his arms and legs, but he is going to be okay. He's at home taking it easy," Jack finished. Jane smiled wearily in relief and they continued towards school together, content to walk in quiet while their parents filled the silence. They met Ginny outside of her house. She was also with her mother, and both Jack and Jane received a big hug from Ginny's mother for their part in her rescue.

Jane thought back to the previous night and shuddered. She and Ginny had managed to stay on Church Road, with the hordes of emergency services that had arrived, and wait for Ginny's mother and David to be rescued. Afterwards they had all travelled to hospital together for a check-up. Jack had gone on ahead earlier, in the first ambulance with his badly injured father. But everyone met up again at the hospital and talked rapidly in between visits from doctors and being subjected to various tests. David and Alfred remained silent as much as they could, only speaking when pressed, and then with as few syllables as possible. Jane could see David was ashamed, but she didn't quite know what to say to help him. She had a feeling he would never get over the night's events. As for Alfred Jane didn't know what to say, and before she could think of anything, her mother turned up and ushered her home.

"Did you hear about Mr Cunningham?" Ginny interrupted Jane's recollection. Ginny was not a great believer in quiet, and soon everyone was speaking at the same time, however as Jane talked to Jack and Ginny, she picked up snippets of their parent's conversation and gradually pieced all the information together.

Mr Cunningham had been caught by the police, as they had arrived on the scene last night, trying to drive away in Ginny's mother's car. He was naked, and had a lot of scratches and cuts, and was somewhat reluctant to say how he had come to be in that condition. He was now under police guard at the hospital as the main suspect, although the police weren't sure what crime he had committed. Ginny's mother's car had been impounded as evidence along with her Louis Vuitton bag. Alfred had been taken into care by social services and was now at an undisclosed location. Alfred Thatcher was officially missing and his home was being examined by police forensics. Apparently, the police sniffer dogs had refused to enter his house and so the police were taking the house apart, floorboard by floorboard.

The statement that the police had released for the press stated that, there had been an incident near Church Road in Middle Gratestone. An out of control dog, suspected of being an illegal breed, might still be on the loose in the area and residents were advised to remain indoors. One man, suspected of being the owner of the dog, had been arrested and was being held in the hospital under police guard. The incident was under investigation by the police and further details would be released when available.

Jack walked between the two girls for the rest of the journey to school and they continued to talk about the night's events. The girls each hooked an arm into the crook of Jack's elbow and leaned into him as they walked, although Jack couldn't fail to notice that Jane appeared to be leaning in just a little bit more than Ginny. The headmaster was waiting with the police at the school main door underneath the banner that read '100 years of shame.' He greeted the group in a serious yet concerned manner and introduced them to the police officers.

And so, began a day of interviews and endless questions, during which Jane was not sure whether she was believed or not. And as the questions probed deeper, and Jane tried to explain what had happened, she began to wonder if it was possible that Alfred could be as innocent and unthreatening as he seemed.

Books by the Author

From the Middle Gratestone Series:
The Shame of Middle Gratestone (Book One)
Haunted by Death (Book Two)

16529997R00146

Printed in Great Britain
by Amazon